Corridors
of Death

Also by Ruth Dudley Edwards

Corridors of Death

Ruth Dudley Edwards

Poisoned Pen Press

Copyright © 1981, 2007 by Ruth Dudley Edwards
First U.S. Trade Paperback Edition 2007

10 9 8 7 6 5 4 3 2 1

Library of Congress Catalog Card Number: 2006940853

ISBN: 978-1-59058-434-7 Trade Paperback

Poisoned Pen Press
6962 E. First Ave., Ste. 103
Scottsdale, AZ 85251
www.poisonedpenpress.com
info@poisonedpenpress.com

Printed in the United States of America

To Patrick Cosgrave,
who suggested it,
and
to my friends in the Civil Service,
who deserve better

Monday Afternoon

Chapter One

The Chancellor of the Exchequer summed up the discussion with a smoothness and wit which efficiently masked his fury. His invitation to the assembled industrialists, trades unionists, ministerial colleagues and civil servants to adjourn for drinks and lunch concluded the meeting and was swiftly followed by a well-bred stampede of aching bladders in the direction of the gentlemen's lavatory. Amiss knew his place as a civil servant—and a junior one at that—too well to seek early relief, and trailed behind the less urgent cases to the outer room, where he moved swiftly towards the drinks table. It was one thing to yield to his seniors in the rush for the bog, but he was damned if he was about to allow his sense of propriety to extend to holding back from grabbing the quickest and largest drink available. After what he—as a member of the Department of Conservation's team of officials—had suffered that morning, he needed what solace he could find.

'Embarrassing business, wasn't it?' said a pleased Treasury voice at his side, and, with suppressed irritation, Amiss directed at the smirking face of Peregrine Pryce-Jones the appropriate bland smile, with its implicit refusal to admit that his own Secretary of State had this time made not an ass, but an egregious ass of himself—in full view of the most distinguished industrial-political group in the British Isles. 'Gin and tonic?' he offered, by way of distraction, and with it a hastily invented problem on which the Department of Conservation could use some wise but informal advice from a rising young economist.

As Pryce-Jones dithered fluently on, 'on the one hand' giving way to 'on the other', sentences beginning 'There are four points to be considered here' inevitably yielding up four and only four points, each concisely stated, each unassailable, each promising some kind of conclusion, while the sum of their parts yielded nothing remotely involving a commitment, Amiss allowed his eyes to stray around the room in search of his immediate master. Sir Nicholas, Permanent Secretary of the Department, and engineer of the 'embarrassing business', was nowhere in evidence. Amiss, his Private Secretary, considered briefly whether this could conceivably be due to shame at the confusion to which his unaccountable malice had reduced first the Secretary of State for Conservation and then the entire group, but dismissed the idea with a snort. The snort struck the wrong note among the compliant grunts with which he had been punctuating the Treasury man's cogent exposition. Pryce-Jones, suddenly recognizing that his enthusiasm for his subject had led him to waste ten valuable minutes on a youth whose only possible importance was as a source of inside information, but who had neatly evaded a gossip about the morning's events, discreetly swivelled his own eyeballs under cover of a swig of his drink, discovered someone with whom he must just have a word, and disappeared across the room.

Too junior to be properly entitled to start a conversation with any of the national figures present and too tender from the morning's *débâcle* to leave himself open to any more snide remarks from colleagues in other departments ('What's got into your minister, old boy?'), Amiss headed for the lavatory. He reckoned it should by now have received the worst of the onslaughts of the famous. He felt ill-used when he found himself leaving simultaneously with the Chancellor, who, he feared, might well identify him as one of the group of officials guilty by association with Sir Nicholas. The Chancellor, however, true to form, chatted amiably and inconsequentially as they stood at adjacent urinals. Not for the first time Amiss thought how inhibiting it must be for the mighty to find themselves exposing their private parts in the company of those so inferior in status and sensibilities that curiosity might impel them to take a swift appraising peek. He had often wondered if it was that consideration or simple prudery that made Sir Nicholas head for the cubicle on such occasions.

They re-entered the room and the Chancellor headed off with a wide smile and an arm already poised for a democratic hugging of the shoulders of some influential trades unionists. Amiss again surveyed the group in search of Sir Nicholas's pinched face. Unsuccessful once more, he investigated the conference room next door and, at a loss for other ideas, returned to the drinks table in time to snatch another large one before the drift into lunch.

Depression had gripped him by now. If the old bastard had gone back to the office Amiss would get a bollicking for staying to lunch. If he didn't stay to lunch it was equally inevitable that the shit would turn up to it late and be furious to find no Private Secretary. He wouldn't even have the consolation of a decent meal—this group's preoccupation with public-expenditure cuts ensured that the civil-service caterers would provide the Grade Four lunch, normally reserved for gatherings with neither political nor industrial clout. Sitting at the end of the minions' table, wading through a grey and mottled soup, gristle in gravy with powdered potatoes, and a sweating cheese, and listening half-heartedly to an animated discussion on forecasting models being held between two alert young officials across the table, Amiss was conscious of the roars of insincere laughter from the top table. Would that the multitude could observe how the leaders of management, workers and the political parties (who within minutes would be giving a press conference denouncing each other) comported themselves in private. If they could hear Alf Shaw of the Plastics Extrusion Workers' Union calling his main industrialist opponent 'Puffy', while the Secretary of State for Energy massaged the arm of the large lady from the Conserve Our Natural Resources Association, they might become as disenchanted as Amiss felt as his meal congealed in a stomach already taxed by a hangover, his nervous panic of the morning and his deepening gloom at the horrors he would face during the afternoon.

The cheese was still glistening on his plate, and his neighbours displaying signs of some emotion over certain aspects of econometrics, when a security guard slid through the door and whispered to the Chancellor of the Exchequer. The Chancellor rose and surveyed the room. 'Gentlemen,' he began and, hastily, after a throat clearing from the large lady, 'Lady and gentlemen. I have distressing news.' Amiss had just realized that the pallor of the speaker's face indicated something more than a new disappointment about the money-supply figures when he heard him continue. 'I regret to have to tell you that Sir Nicholas Clark has been found dead. I must ask you all to remain in this room until further notice.'

As the Chancellor sped towards the doorway, Amiss found that whatever emotion he might otherwise have felt at the news of his superior's demise was completely overlaid by a new panic about protocol. Shouldn't a Private Secretary be at his master's side even if that master was a corpse? Or would that appear pushy and therefore likely to be noted down against him on his next personnel report? Christ, he couldn't be expected to be *au fait* with any precedents for this. Permanent Secretaries didn't die at work. They retired at sixty, pink-cheeked and ready to supplement their index-linked pensions with a brace of directorships. God, what had the civil service reduced him to in only four years? Career prospects, at a moment like this? But wasn't that what Sir Nicholas would have wished? He, after all, would have shown only glee if an aircraft containing every official senior to him had crashed with fatal consequences to all on board. Anyway, Amiss loathed Sir Nicholas so much that he would be better off thinking practically rather than letting his real emotions show.

His training reasserted itself, and, with a face displaying controlled distress and concern, he fell to the duty of fielding the questions which those who had spotted him as the man-in-the-know were wittering at him. 'No, Sir Nicholas was in excellent health.'

'Yes, indeed a great tragedy for the Department.' 'Certainly—an appalling shock for his family.' 'Yes, a wife and son.' No one had anything worth saying and he was no better. Of all groups to be faced with a stiff on the doorstep, this had to be one of the least well-fitted. Arguments over the statistics of deaths from hypothermia?—fine. Deaths from pneumoconiosis?—certainly. There were no better people to utter appropriately compassionate noises about paper deaths. But an actual corpse—and one which seemed likely to postpone the press conference, and even then deny the lead performers their histrionics?—that was something for which they didn't have the precedents either.

'Very distressing' was beginning to give way to 'Well, really! Is there any need for us to remain any longer?' when the Chancellor re-entered, now green rather than white. 'Lady and gentlemen,' he said, 'I regret that I must ask you to remain here until the police arrive.' Stemming the hubbub of questions and complaints, he continued flatly. 'Sir Nicholas has been murdered. We will all be required to assist the police with their enquiries.'

Chapter Two

Amiss had always dreamed of being present at an event so unexpected that it reduced a group of professional articulators to
appalled silence, but murder hadn't featured among his fantasies.
These had tended more to visions of himself leaping on to the
table and telling all those present what a collection of self-satisfied old farts they were. Even if his was not a central role, at least
he now knew that even they could be dumbfounded; not even
Alf or Puffy could produce a suitable word. Amiss could only
suppose that they were all now engaged in assessing the effect
this event was likely to have on their reputations. Presumably,
if the murderer had been found, all of them would have been
let go; they must therefore be suspects. That suggested that Sir
Nicholas had been killed very close to this room. Since almost no
one working regularly in this building knew him, the suspects in
this room had a head-start. It would have been a different matter
had he been found dead in his own department. Amiss could
off-hand think of about two dozen likely murderers there and
about a hundred others who would have cheered them on.

The police arrived while Amiss was occupied in drawing up
a rough mental list of the prime suspects present. His conclusions had such horrendous implications that he could feel only
sympathy for the policemen just now crossing the threshold
of what must be a grade-one hairy investigation. One Cabinet
minister, one junior minister, one major industrialist, one senior
civil servant—Jesus, Scotland Yard would need the heavy mob for

this. It wasn't just that they were people in the public eye who were nervous of their reputations. There wasn't one of them who hadn't arrived at his present position through his ability to obfuscate while appearing to clarify. Some of them had had thirty or more years' experience of deflecting straight questions by a combination of bluff, clichés and charm. Amiss could spot only three people in the room in addition to himself who were inexperienced enough to tell someone their names without prior calculation. The police would fare better at a coven of Wittgenstein's apostles.

The uniformed vanguard were discreet enough, but nothing compared to the three grave-looking, nattily suited men who slid quietly into the room after them. Well, thought Amiss, they would hardly send the Riot Squad. But wasn't it a bit sneaky that they weren't even wearing black shiny toecaps and blue shirts? Admittedly they did look relatively fit—a dead give-away in this company. Amiss saw one of the younger pair give a quick glance around the room and betray by a start his recognition of a number of familiar faces. The oldest of the three walked up to the Chancellor—already on his feet and wearing a look of relief—and, after a murmured consultation, proceeded to the end of the room and cleared his throat. 'Good afternoon. My name is Detective Superintendent James Milton and I am in charge of this enquiry. I am sorry that you have been detained for so long already. I recognize that you are all busy people, but I fear I must ask you to show even greater patience. If you wish to send any urgent messages, Detective Sergeant Pike will arrange to have them transmitted. Detective Sergeant Romford and I will use the conference room next door as an office. We would like to see you there one by one. Perhaps the Chancellor would kindly accompany us now?'

As the babble of questions broke out, Milton shook his head, expressed his regrets about his inability to answer them, and, accompanied by Romford, left with the Chancellor meekly in tow. Amiss waited his turn to add to Pike's list of messages a telephone number and the information that he would be having a long lunch-break and sat back to continue his speculations.

It became quickly apparent that the pecking-order was being observed irreproachably. The Secretary of State for Energy was summoned after ten minutes, and as the afternoon was whiled away with subdued gossip, paper work and *The Times* crossword, senior politicians were followed by the President of the Confederation of British Industry, the General Secretary of the Trades Union Congress and a succession of lesser figures. It was all as efficient and protocol-conscious as a Buckingham Palace dinner. Either Scotland Yard superintendents carried books on etiquette or the superintendent had found an adviser. Amiss was too well aware of his lowly status to be surprised when he found himself the last to be called.

He found Milton at the head of the conference table, and looking decidedly less composed—to a degree that could not be explained solely by the steady four hours it had taken him to get through about eighteen luminaries and their attendant staff. His lean face was set in lines of strain, his dark hair was rumpled and he kept nervously disassembling and reassembling his expensive pen. Amiss felt sufficiently sorry for him to go out of his way to offer information about himself. He saw more than a flicker of interest in Milton's face when he explained that he had been Clark's Private Secretary, followed by a decided look of relief when he proffered a few incautious words about Sir Nicholas's general unpopularity.

After they had taken a formal statement of his movements between the end of the meeting and the discovery of the body, Milton sent Romford back to Scotland Yard to get his notes typed. He looked fixedly at Amiss. 'Listen,' he said, 'I'm in need of help and you're in a position to give it.' Amiss drew breath to make polite noises of denial, but Milton cut him short. 'I've sat here for four hours taking statements from people who have overwhelmed me with unctuous drivel about the fine qualities of the deceased. They have given me not one single fact I didn't drag out of them. They saw nothing, heard nothing and can think of no reason why anyone would murder such a fine public servant. Nearly half of them, God help me, have made helpful suggestions about muggers and tramps—despite the fact that I have explained to each of them that Sir Nicholas was killed in the gentlemen's lavatory on this, the twenty-seventh floor of Embankment Tower, an office block which boasts four sober security guards and an apparently water-tight entry-pass system. Not only, it seems, did you know the man better than anyone else, you are the first to have offered me anything other than pious crap. You can point me at likely suspects, help me to understand motives and explain to me what goes on in bloody Whitehall. And what's more, you have a cast-iron alibi unless you and the Chancellor of the Exchequer are involved in a conspiracy.'

Amiss liked this policeman. But then there was the ethos of the civil service. He thought about breaking ranks, ratting, letting the side down, being over-zealous, bringing the service into disrepute and all the other things he would be doing if he gave Milton the kind of cooperation he deserved. He thought about his career—blotting his copybook, demonstrating poor judgement, displaying disloyalty towards colleagues—all the accusations he would be open to if he were found acting as a copper's nark. He thought of the semi-helpful information he could give Milton if he left out the bits that might be traced back to him. Then he thought about his self-respect and his sympathy for the under-dog. If ever there was an under-dog it was this poor sod, who was going to make a long, slow and tedious balls of the whole business if someone didn't give him a helping hand. Milton didn't look away while Amiss was thinking all this through. Amiss liked that too.

'All right,' he said, 'I'll give you the dirt, and without any reservations, on two conditions. You guarantee that none of my colleagues ever knows where you got your information from—and that means meeting me when and where I suggest—and you compensate me for the risk I'm running by keeping me daily in touch with your investigation, thus satisfying my curiosity.'

'What risk could you possibly be running that would entitle you to be kept informed of the progress of a confidential police investigation?' asked Milton, covering his grin with a stern copper look. 'The same sort of risk you would run if you pointed the finger at a crooked colleague,' said Amiss. Milton looked him in the eyes for a minute and the grin broke. 'Done,' he said and held out his hand.

Monday Evening

Chapter Three

They met a couple of hours later in a seedy curry-house of Amiss's choice—well away from Whitehall and staffed by waiters with limited English. Milton had had time to throw a few noncommittal scraps to the slavering pack of newshounds, go back to the Yard for consultations with superiors, arrange for the processing of the statements and the routine checking of alibis, check that the preliminary pathology report had come up with nothing helpful and dismiss his sergeants for the evening. Amiss had had time to show his face in his office, confirm to colleagues that he had undergone only a routine interview with the police, make a few telephone calls, talk to the Deputy Secretary who had already taken over responsibility for Clark's work, and ensure that papers for immediate action were being dispatched to the proper quarters. There was no need to cancel any of Sir Nicholas's appointments; the civil-service machine was more than capable of coping with sudden death, however scandalous. Sir Nicholas's meetings and speeches from tomorrow onwards would be dealt with by his temporary successor, Douglas Sanders, who would by morning have digested enough briefing material to enable him to behave as if he had been in the job for years. Sanders's responsibilities would be similarly taken over, and the only sufferers would be the poor devils who were now required within a few hours to expand existing briefing to cope with the newfound ignorance of some of their superiors.

Sanders dismissed Amiss with an approving nod and Amiss mentally saw a tick on his personnel report under the section headed 'Ability to cope with pressure'. He hurried off with relief to the twilight environment of the Star of India, where Milton was already lurking in a distant corner. 'Ah, Robert,' Milton hailed him. 'Sit down and have a drink, and tell me why, at a moment of personal tragedy, you are smirking all over your face.'

'It's the masterly way in which you employ my Christian name to denote our new status as unofficial colleagues, James. It is James, not Jim, I trust. Civil servants don't like diminutives; they're considered vulgar.'

'God Almighty, don't tell me that the use of Christian names is another civil-service mystery. It's very simple with us. You just call everyone your senior "sir". And I'm afraid it is Jim.'

'I can see you've got a lot to learn. To put it simply, if you've got no other evidence to go on, the use of the Christian name is the key to finding out a man's status and prospects. Thus, if you are sitting with an official of immense importance and two men enter the room—one young and spotty, one middle-aged and distinguished looking—you may assume that the former works for the latter. Then you hear young and spotty address your host as Alaric and middle-aged and distinguished address him as Mr Snodgrass. This means that young and spotty is a high-flyer, has a good degree—probably from Oxbridge—and has come into the service at the bottom of the administrative ladder. The other poor fellow, who may still outrank him, is a decent soul who has worked his way up the executive ranks but has little hope of ever attaining real power. Conversely, your high-flyer will probably be addressed by his minions by his Christian name—because he can afford to be seen to be democratic—while the other honest fellow, who has been obliged to spend years grovelling to his superiors only to be overtaken by people half his age, will cling to his few privileges and will be addressed as Mr Blenkinsop by all who work for him.'

Milton's stunned look touched Amiss's heart and he broke off his discourse. 'Sorry. You've enough troubles without my digressing on the anthropology of the civil service. I've dug up some information for you, but I want yours first.'

They paused to order a meal and then Milton leant forward warily. 'So far we know that Sir Nicholas Clark died in the cubicle of the lavatory after a heavy blow to the base of the skull from a small steel abstract sculpture, the top part of which provided a useful handle.'

'He'd have liked that. Always fancied himself a bit of an aesthete. But who in God's name was carrying round with him an object like that? You don't get many modern-art enthusiasts at IGGY.'

'IGGY?'

'Sorry. The group is called the Industry and Government Group, and we do go in for disrespectful acronyms.' At the look on Milton's face Amiss hastily yielded the floor.

'No one was carrying it about with him. It happened to be conveniently placed on a stand about six feet away from the lavatory. You must have seen it. Two interweaving circles on a round base.'

'Not ...?'

'Yes. The piece entitled "Reconciliation".'

'I'm beginning to like this murderer more and more,' said Amiss gloomily. 'It's affecting my motivation.'

'Believe me,' said Milton. 'There are heavy odds against our man being either a prankster with a keen sense of the ridiculous or a zealot determined to make the world a better place by ridding it of someone who, I infer, was a blot on the civil service escutcheon. It's very rarely the motive is anything worthier than greed or fear.'

'All right. Go on.'

'Sir Nicholas was discovered at 1.55 by an Embankment Tower Accommodation Officer summoned to investigate the mysterious immovability of the cubicle door. By the time the police doctor arrived it was possible only to estimate the time of death as being between approximately 12.45 and 1.15. There were no finger-prints on the top part of the sculpture and only a few half-hearted smudges on the base. Anyway, that was largely covered in blood and ...'

'Yes, yes. Don't put me off my Chicken Biryani. Obviously any prints you identify will be those of people wholly unconnected with IGGY.'

'Right. The murderer used one of those little linen towels laid on, I understand, on the days when there are important meetings in the conference room.'

'Why was the cubicle door immovable anyway? Wouldn't he have toppled forward when he was struck?'

'It looks as if his murderer hit him as he pushed the cubicle door inwards. He would then certainly have fallen forward. As far as we can see the murderer then half closed the door and leaned the body against it so that Sir Nicholas's weight pushed it shut. There are no gaps under those doors, so nothing was visible. Anyone who tried it would have found it resistant to pushing. That's why it took so long to discover the body.'

'Would the murderer have had to be particularly strong?'

'No, he wouldn't. The preliminary pathology report is of little help. It rules out only people of below average height and weight or the excessively tall. That excludes only half a dozen of the people who attended the IGGY meeting.' Milton screwed his face up at the unpalatable acronym and took a gulp of lager.

'So far, so bad. Have you managed to rule many out by checking alibis?'

'Someone's doing an exhaustive check now, but it looks as though it's down to eight, all of whom can account for their movements but can't produce witnesses for all of them. Virtually everyone except two of the civil servants went to the lavatory some time during that half hour.'

'It would be civil servants. They develop highly trained bladders to save them ever missing any part of a meeting lest their departmental interests suffer from their absence. So who's on the present short list?'

Milton pushed a list over to him.

Norman Grewe, Chairman, Industrial Electronics
Gerald Hunter, Secretary of State for Energy
Martin Jenkins, President, Fitters' Union
Harvey Nixon, Secretary of State for Conservation
Richard Parkinson, Assistant Secretary, Department of Conservation
Alfred Shaw, President, Plastics Extrusion Workers' Union
Archibald Stafford, Chairman, Plastics Conversion Company
William Wells, Parliamentary Under-Secretary of State, Department of Conservation

'Terrific,' said Amiss. 'Our department provides three— Nixon, Wells and Parkinson. The government—already shaky and with a small majority—provides three as well—Hunter, and Nixon and Wells again.'

'Obviously we want to minimize the dislocation to government. I've had a lot of heavy breathing from my superiors about this already. The real difficulty now is to find motives, because if the eight are to be believed, there wasn't one amongst them who had even the most rudimentary of reasons to want to see Sir Nicholas off. Grewe, Jenkins and Hunter claim nodding acquaintance only and the others talked about him as a friend rather than a colleague.'

'I can't help you with the nodding acquaintances,' said Amiss grimly, 'but if three strong motives and one weak one are of any use, you'd better get out your notebook.'

Chapter Four

'Did any single one of those who attended IGGY this morning tell you anything about the fiasco which revealed that Harvey Nixon, while presenting a paper on an aspect of his department's policy, hadn't the faintest idea what he was talking about?'

'Need you ask?'

'No. It's a complicated story which I spent some time this evening disentangling with the unsuspecting help of the Private Secretary network within Whitehall. You ought to know that Private Secretaries hear everything, see everything and tell only each other most of it. The fiasco itself was inexplicable as it occurred, unless you accept that Sir Nicholas was prepared to sacrifice his future career entirely for the sake of his malice towards Nixon and Wells. His machinations over the past few days make me assume that he had totally flipped. We'll have to start with the characters of the two politicians involved—Nixon and Wells. What do you know about either of them?'

'Very little. I saw so many people, and so quickly, this afternoon that they're all a blur. But I know that Wells is some kind of junior minister with a radical reputation.'

'You need to get his status clear. A Parliamentary Under-Secretary of State is known for convenience—even in official documents—by the acronym PUSS. And that about sums up the general view of what his role should be. Our department has one Secretary of State, two Ministers of State, each of whom is basically his deputy for half the work, and each of them has a PUSS. The

PUSS is normally without power, influence or honour, unless he happens to be very lucky in his superiors. His job is to stand in for ministers on unimportant occasions, see difficult but uninfluential deputations, do what he is told and shut up otherwise. I've even heard the PUSS described as being in office mainly for young officials to practise their burgeoning minister-controlling skills on. Every Whitehall civil servant's and most senior ministers' nightmare is a PUSS who gets too big for his boots and starts showing initiative, reminding ministers of manifesto commitments and trying to score at their expense in the party. Wells is a pain in the arse to everyone who works in the Department of Conservation.'

'Why? Because he's independent-minded?'

'No. We're not that bad. Independence of mind may often be an irritant, but it takes more than that to incur actual dislike. Wells is disliked because he is ambitious and unprincipled, while setting himself up as a principled man surrounded by time-servers. His radicalism gives him a power-base within his party which makes him difficult to sack; so he loses no opportunity of upstaging his colleagues and showing his contempt for civil servants, whom he never ceases to treat as subverters of the will of the people. Hardly fair—most of the time we merely try to enact the wishes of the Cabinet. We may be seen as the sinister undemocratic secret rulers of the country, but in fact we're usually pretty loyal to our governments. That bugger treats us like the secret police and fuddy-duddy obscurantists by turns. And when you get choked off with the unhelpfulness you are likely to meet during this enquiry, remember that civil servants, too, have to put up with a lot of shit. Pass the chutney.'

'Right. I've got Wells clear. Now Nixon always seems from press accounts to be a modest and competent sort of fellow.'

'Modest he is. Competent he's not. He's a prime example of the power of the civil-service machine. He was made a senior minister for two good reasons. First, he was intensely loyal, and could be relied on to do anything the Prime Minister told him to do. Second, as a Scot, he helps to maintain a regional balance within the Cabinet.'

'Surely that wouldn't be enough to compensate for lack of ability?'

'My God, have you any idea how many conflicting pressures a Prime Minister faces in getting a Cabinet together? Lobbies, regional *amour propre*, left/right/centre balance to be struck, no class or profession to dominate, personal debts of gratitude to be paid, magnanimity to be shown by the inclusion of erstwhile opponents, and more. When all that's been taken account of, a Prime Minister would appoint to a vacant senior post someone who couldn't read and write if his loyalty could be counted on. As long as you can scrawl a signature, you don't need to be literate, let alone intelligent, to be a Cabinet Minister. Sorry—correction. You need to be able to read your speeches, but you'll certainly never have to write them or anything else if you don't want to.'

Milton wiped his brow, but whether at these distressing revelations about the practicalities of government life or at the heat of the Meat Vindaloo he had incautiously ordered, Amiss couldn't be sure.

'Look at it the other way, Jim. Even if a Cabinet could be chosen on sheer merit, you'd be lucky to find a dozen people in the ruling party who could succeed at all aspects of the job. You need the stamina of a horse. Between party meetings, constituency responsibilities, House of Commons debates, routine ministerial duties, major speeches laying down government policy, Cabinet meetings and Cabinet committees, you're lucky to have a couple of nights a week when you get home by ten. And even then, like every other night, you have one or two large boxes full of paper which, in theory, you digest and comment sensibly on. It's an impossible load as it is, the way we run government. It's almost unbearable when, as now, a small majority means that the minister has to be present to vote on even unimportant motions day and night in the House of Commons.'

'I'm beginning to feel sorry for Nixon.'

'So you should. A decent, compassionate M.P. Quite a good speaker when he knows what he's talking about. Ambitions admittedly rather above his abilities, but for him most of the consequences of holding office turn out to be harassment round the clock, sniping in the House and perpetual terror of being asked detailed questions about policies he hasn't initiated and hasn't had time to grasp. On top of that, he has to nurse a marginal constituency in Glasgow.'

'Why don't people like that tell the Prime Minister that he can stuff his jobs?'

'Because of loyalty or ambition, and because the glamour of office makes up for a lot. Everywhere you go you have cars to carry you, lavish offices to work in, minions—and intelligent ones at that—at your beck and call. People call you "minister" and treat you with deference. Play your cards right and you'll end up in the House of Lords with a meal ticket and a platform for life. Only an exceptional man would give up all that for a half share in a scrubby little office in the House of Commons, a drop in salary of seventy per cent and a reduction in staff to half a secretary.'

'I understand,' said Milton, wondering if he would himself have the integrity to turn down the Commissioner's job, arse-licking of politicians and pussy-footing with the press notwithstanding.

'The late Sir Nicholas Clark despised Nixon and hated Wells. It looks as if last week he decided to nobble them both. It wasn't a difficult job for him, because, as I said, he was prepared to risk his own career in the process. It merely required him to bypass a system of checks and balances which ensures most of the time that people turn up in the right places with the right kind of material.'

If Milton had been alert so far, he was quivering now.

'Nixon would normally have attended IGGY, but he had a whole weekend of constituency appointments—in Glasgow, remember. It was some local party anniversary or other, and he had been advised by Sir Nicholas that another minister could attend this meeting since it was unlikely to be controversial. He left the office early last Friday evening intending not to return until mid-morning on Monday. He had asked his Private

Secretary specifically to put in his despatch box only the most urgent papers. On some pretext Sir Nicholas borrowed the IGGY papers from Nixon's office, saying the minister wouldn't be needing them. The relevant Minister of State—that's the next level down, remember—was away, so Wells, the PUSS, was going to stand in for Nixon. He was cock-a-hoop at the prospect of performing in front of the Chancellor and attracting more attention in twenty minutes than he could normally have hoped for in two years' hard work. He had spent days demanding more and more briefing for the meeting, at which he was to present for discussion a paper on department policy on paper recycling. His introductory speech was drafted by a civil servant, savaged, rewritten, denounced, rewritten and then finally touched up by Wells himself on Friday. He also disappeared in the early evening, papers in hand, smirk on face, leaving a train of cursing officials in his wake hoping that he would over-reach himself and come a cropper on Monday.'

'Don't tell me. Sir Nicholas fixed it so Nixon had to turn up to IGGY unbriefed. But how?'

'He used his rank and traded on the trust any politician or civil servant puts in the integrity and reliability of a Permanent Secretary. He rang up his opposite number in the Treasury and conveyed the worrying news that the TUC were going to mount a major protest against some hitherto uncontroversial aspect of the paper. Mightn't the Chancellor feel in the circumstances that the Secretary of State should be there rather than an inexperienced junior of juniors? It wouldn't look too good at the Press Conference, would it? "Christ, no," said his opposite number, haring in to the Chancellor, starting a panic and getting back to Sir Nicholas to say "retrieve your man at all costs and cancel the PUSS". "Don't worry, my dear chap," says Judas. "I'll see to all that." Exit Treasury-man with a sigh of relief, leaving to his old reliable friend the job of passing on the news.'

'What did he do?' asked Milton in fascination. 'Nothing?'

'Better than that. He rang Nixon on Sunday night, catching him in the middle of a constituency dinner in Glasgow and about to make a major speech. He told him he had to be on parade at IGGY at 10.00 next morning. God knows what excuses he made for the delay in letting him know—blamed it on the Private Secretary, probably. Nixon flaps. No way of getting back to London more than half an hour before the meeting starts. No briefing. "Tsch, tsch," says Sir Nicholas, "how surprising that you haven't got the papers. But the Chancellor was most insistent that you should be there. Don't worry. I'll meet your plane in the morning with all the bumf and you'll have time to scan the brief and the speech and discuss them with me before we arrive at the meeting.'"

'And I suppose he didn't turn up.'

'Right. Although he did send Nixon's Private Secretary with the briefing and a speech. They weren't to know that it was the wrong speech, which Sir Nicholas had manufactured himself. It was about paper recycling, yes. But it was redolent with misunderstandings of the issues, mis-statements of what was in the paper to be discussed, wrong statistics, bits of Greek and French—neither of which Nixon can pronounce. By the time Nixon had got to his car, what-the-helled his secretary, looked despairingly at the huge pile of paper which he was supposed to be able to discuss intelligently, he had time, one assumes, only to give the most cursory glance at the speech. It was the first item on the IGGY agenda and the poor bastard never had a chance. He made a shambles of reading the speech and then went completely to pieces when the few present who knew something about the subject started to question him on the mis-statements and wrong facts in it.'

'But surely he could have explained what had happened?'

'Government doesn't work like that. Haven't you ever seen press reports about ministers being castigated in the House because they signed a letter with an error in it? It doesn't matter that every week they sign hundreds of letters they've no time to read. The pretence is kept up that they know everything that's going on. They are responsible if some Clerical Officer they've never met cocks up an official statistic. It's known as ministerial accountability. Of course it's nonsense, but it's hallowed nonsense. No. He had no option but to soldier on and rely on whatever help he had to hand. In theory his political colleagues would try to protect him in discussion and his civil servants would pass him helpful notes when he didn't know the answers to questions.'

'Well, didn't they?'

'They would have. But Sir Nicholas had arranged it so that those present were himself and two others, Parkinson and me, neither of whom knew a blind thing about the subject. Sir Nicholas ignored the signals from Nixon, and at the crucial stage of the discussion left the room for ten minutes. Normally there would be someone there to act as a long-stop, but on this occasion no one was equipped to field the simplest question. By the time Sir Nicholas got back the Chancellor had managed to pass on to the next item with some mumble about pressure of time and Nixon was sitting there deathly pale, having seen himself revealed in front of a key group of his peers and superiors as a bumbling incompetent. And Sir Nicholas looked at him and smiled.'

Milton ordered another round of drinks. 'Funny terminology you lot use—long-stops and all that. My sergeant showed me one of the telephone messages he passed on this afternoon—"Hope to be back in office before close of play."'

Amiss laughed. 'You can't avoid it in the civil service. It's an integral part of our language, possibly because it's conveniently vague. "Close of play", for instance, means some time between 5.30 and 7.00, depending on what time the recipient is likely to knock off. To put a specific time on it is rather frowned on. Gentlemen don't leave at a regular time; only minions do that. We also talk about straight bats, opening bats, sticky wickets, bouncers and balls going wide.'

'Are you all cricket fanatics?'

'Oh, no. Probably very few of us are. It's not even consciously figurative any more. There was an attempted revolt by soccer enthusiasts in my office some time ago—memos going round with half-time, full-time, off-side, own goals and so on, but they didn't catch on. Officials have to cope with political change too often to be prepared to compromise on what they regard as really sacrosanct—language and customs.'

Milton considered this for a moment. 'I know the score on that now,' he said. 'Let's leave the gentlemen and get back to the players: where was Wells while Nixon's balls were being driven to the boundary? Or is that too laboured?'

'A bit. And anyway, Nixon was batting. I suppose you could say Wells was watching from the pavilion, having been shoved out of the team in a humiliating way. He had arrived that morning already bearing his share of personal troubles, also precipitated by Sir Nicholas, who, being always in touch with gossip about ministers' private lives, had known very well that Wells was spending the weekend with his mistress on the pretext of a departmental conference.'

'You go along with that sort of cover-up?'

'Not directly. But we tell lies about ministerial whereabouts if we have to. We're servants, remember. We may wear dark suits and talk with posh accents, but our job is to keep our masters happy. We draw the line at pimping for them, but we certainly would be expected to pass on any messages they gave us. Anyway, Sir Nicholas, knowing that, had the happy thought of ringing up Wells's home, identifying himself and asking to speak to him. When Mrs Wells mentioned the conference, Sir Nicholas apparently denied all knowledge of it, expressed surprise, managed to arouse all her suspicions and rang off. According to his Private Secretary, the earful Wells got when he rang home just before this morning's meeting would have left a lesser careerist in bits, but the thought of his triumph to come carried him through. Until, that is, he found himself put out of his seat at the conference table to make way for Nixon. He was condescendingly invited to stay and had a bird's-eye view of Nixon's collapse from a seat at the other side of the room. As an observer, he could do nothing at all to retrieve the situation. And remember that in this unjust world his reputation would have taken a dive purely by association with Nixon's failure.'

'Anything else is going to be an anti-climax after this,' said Milton faintly. 'But I suppose you'd better go on to the other motive and a half.'

Chapter Five

'The next best motive is Archibald Stafford's.'

'Is this going to be as complicated as the other two?' asked Milton, miming coffee at the waiter across the room. 'I'm beginning to hanker after something simple.'

'Well, I can skip the technicalities if you like, and confine to the basic minimum my account of how Sir Nicholas set out to wreck Stafford's career.'

'Please do. It's late already, and since I can't tell anyone about our deal I've the job tomorrow of trying to extract from Nixon and Wells the information you've already given me. Bloody awkward, unless they believe in the god-like intuition of the super-sleuth. Not that I'm complaining, of course.'

'I had some understanding of why he hated Nixon and Wells—contempt and ethical revulsion respectively—but why he should have had it in for poor old Stafford is still beyond me. They were at school together, they've had regular social contact ever since—lunches and so on—and I would have put them down as relatively close friends.'

'Is Stafford a successful industrialist?'

'It depends on what you call successful.' And hastily, seeing Milton's face contort at the prospect of equivocation so late in the evening, Amiss added: 'That is, he's risen to the top of a large and prosperous company, and if he isn't pointed to as one of the country's top ten management whizz-kids, he's certainly well liked and respected by the Establishment. Over the years

Sir Nicholas brought him on to all sorts of government advisory committees, and he was useful enough on them to be nominated to the great heights of IGGY with a knighthood an almost certain reward. Everything was going well for him until last year, when his company applied in the normal way for a large grant from this department for an expansion and modernization project.'

'And presumably he expected to have Sir Nicholas's backing?'

'Certainly. Nothing wrong with that. The project would be examined objectively by staff seconded from outside the service, but it could only be a help to know that the Permanent Secretary considered the Executive Chairman to be a dynamic and able leader.'

'Something went wrong?'

'Yes. For Stafford, it couldn't have gone much worse. It wasn't until the other day, when the grant was offered, subject to a management shake-up, that I realized that Sir Nicholas must have been gunning for him all the time. A bit of digging confirmed it.'

'What had he done? Dropped reservations about Stafford in the right ears?'

'More than that, I think. As far as I can see he was instrumental in having an iconoclast, Barnes, chosen as project head. Barnes is an efficient enough chap, but obsessed with the virtues of scientific management and violently opposed to any kind of old-fashioned paternalism—however effective. It's a bit of a joke really, the department employing someone like that when you consider that civil-service interest in management as either an art or a science is zilch. Barnes had a couple of conversations with Sir Nicholas about the case during which, I gather, Barnes was given to understand that much as it pained him to say it, Sir Nicholas thought old Stafford was a good chap but past it. So that was the conclusion Barnes went looking for and that inevitably was what he found. And poor old Stafford, who was well thought of in the department by anyone who had any dealings with him, had complete confidence in his old friend and kept referring Barnes to him as the official who knew most about his management philosophy. Sir Nicholas had indicated to his underlings that he was handling the departmental view on Stafford, so the case for him went by default. By the time Barnes had prepared his report—twenty-four hours before it went to the independent committee which adjudicates on the awarding of grants—it was too late for anybody to retrieve the situation. Plastics Conversion were promised six million pounds in government aid subject to their getting rid of Stafford and a few others.'

'And Stafford isn't so outstanding that he's worth the loss of six million to the company?'

'Certainly the shareholders wouldn't think so.'

'So all that was festering away in Stafford this morning. But he couldn't have known Sir Nicholas was his enemy?'

'No, not necessarily, but it would be interesting to find out if they had had a conversation since the knife went in. Given the manic mood he seems to have been in over the weekend, I wouldn't put it past Sir Nicholas to have told him.'

'Three down. Who had the weak motive?'

'Richard Parkinson. I only call it weak because I can't see why he would have murdered Sir Nicholas now rather than at any other time. He's had reason enough to hate him for years, from all I gather.'

'Don't tell me. He's been trying to ruin his career.'

'Trying? He's done it. Parkinson was a contemporary of Sir Nicholas's at Oxford, although a scientist rather than a classicist. I think they both used to speak at the Union. When he joined the civil service ten years ago he was a successful industrial scientist who took a considerable drop in salary to come into the public sector.'

'Why should he do a silly thing like that?'

'Well, the rumour is that Sir Nicholas advised him to do so on the grounds that he was of such distinction that he would rise effortlessly to the top.'

'And why didn't he?'

'Well, again I'm going on rumour. I've heard it said that when, a couple of years later, he found himself in a bit of a backwater, he was convinced by Sir Nicholas that he should transfer from the scientific to the administrative side of things, where his various talents would all receive recognition. There was an idea abroad in those days, among reformers, that the administrators needed to be shaken up by the introduction of people who really understood technology. Parkinson's industrial experience made him look ideal for imbuing the paper-pushers with a consciousness of what the real world was all about.'

'He didn't succeed, then?'

'He did well enough. From what I've heard he would have ended up at least a Deputy Secretary—that's one from the top— given a break. He didn't have any of the drawbacks that scientists often suffer from in the service, where literacy and articulacy tend to count for more than other qualities. Anyway, he found himself as an Assistant Secretary working directly to Sir Nicholas, who was then an Under Secretary. There he was, with an almost total lack of administrative experience, suffering perpetual embarrassment at the hands of his old pal, who criticized his handling of policy making, parliamentary questions, advice to ministers—everything he did, in short. Whatever he did was wrong.'

'Hang on a minute. I'm getting hopelessly confused about all these secretaries. So far ...' he consulted his notebook, 'I have a Parliamentary Under-Secretary of State—Wells, a Permanent Secretary—the corpse, an Assistant Secretary—Parkinson, and now you're dragging in Under and Deputy Secretaries. On top of all that, you're a Private Secretary. None of you, I presume, does any of the mundane things one normally associates with secretaries, like shorthand and typing.'

Amiss laughed. 'Perish the thought that we might do anything so useful. I'm sorry, I should have explained earlier. It's easy to forget how much difficulty an outsider must have in grasping our antiquated ranking system. Give me a piece of paper and I'll draw you a chart. You won't see any real secretaries on it; they're called Personal Secretaries and they won't show up here.'

'Right,' he said a couple of minutes later. 'Look at this. That's our departmental structure roughly. You can see from the pecking-order that Parkinson is a long way down.'

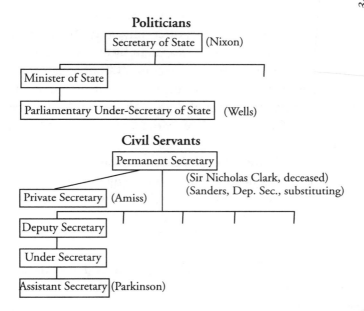

'Where do you fit in? You seem to be out on a limb.'

'I shouldn't be on the chart at all really. I've put myself there at the Permanent Secretary's right hand to clarify things. I'm two ranks below Parkinson at the moment, more or less. If I'm a good boy I'll be made a Principal soon and then I'll be only one below him.'

Milton looked confused. 'A Principal sounds much more important that an Assistant Secretary.'

'Not when you know that the title is short for Principal Clerk—though of course it has nothing nowadays to do with clerical work. All these titles go back at least to the last century. Don't try to understand why we use them—it's easier just to accept.'

Milton ran his eye over the sketch and nodded his comprehension. 'Thanks. I can see that Parkinson hasn't done too well. Why didn't he get out?'

'He left it too late. He had got out of touch with scientific advances of all but the most general sort in his anxiety to learn about his new job.'

'Dear God. Yours seems to be a very cruel world.'

'No, not really. It's often stuffy, often silly, it can be absurdly bureaucratic and it frequently wastes talent by attaching far too much importance to style rather than content. Still, it's got a lot of intelligent, industrious and amusing people who would not be consciously unkind—just thoughtless. And thoughtlessly they left poor old Parkinson to his fate. More and more people got promoted over his head and Sir Nicholas rose to be Permanent Secretary. With his increase in power he was better placed than ever to shake his head when anyone suggested promoting Parkinson. I've heard him referring to Parkinson as a third-rate mind with a second-rate veneer.'

'Did Parkinson know it was Sir Nicholas who was responsible for his condition?'

'He can't have known specifically, but he must have guessed a lot of it. He certainly must have smarted under some of the deft criticisms Sir Nicholas used to make of his work whenever he got the chance—often in memoranda circulated to half a dozen people. He never mentioned him by name, of course. Just made snide references—expressing concern that nothing had been done in this area or that, or surprise at the misjudgement displayed in a draft policy document. Sir Nicholas was very clever,' Amiss sighed. 'I bet *The Times* obituary says he had a first-rate mind.'

'Well, time to draw stumps. I'm taking my third-rate mind home to bed before you tell me that Sir Nicholas was about to have the entire leadership of the TUC arraigned for treason. I don't suppose even you can have a lot more to tell me tomorrow, but in line with our bargain, I'll be here about the same time tomorrow night to fill you in on my day's doings. Here, I'll pay that. Least I can do.'

'If you see me in the department tomorrow, don't for God's sake call me Robert.'

'I'll call you "sir". Nobody ever called me a high flyer.'

Tuesday Morning

Chapter Six

Milton's wife was still asleep when he left at 7.30 the following morning, after five hours' fitful sleep. He doubted if he was to have much conversation with her during the rest of the investigation. Stupid of policemen to marry women they like, he thought dejectedly. The ideal policeman (like the ideal Cabinet Minister, apparently) should be married to a wife so repellent that he would never feel the yearning for some private life. Ann wasn't repellent. Worse, she had a job which took her abroad frequently—she was even now sleeping off jet-lag—and they could go for whole weeks without exchanging much more than written messages of household instructions. He found himself immersed in an increasingly frequent reverie, in which, surrounded by happy, healthy children, he pruned roses, raised exotic vegetables, savoured the smell of baking from the rambling Tudor homestead. There were several routes out of this daydream: his hatred of gardening was exceeded only by Ann's abomination of housekeeping and the terror they both felt of boredom. This time he snapped out of it by recalling the last time he had spent more than ten minutes in the company of a gang of happy, healthy children. Boxing Day. He shuddered.

Boredom certainly wasn't likely to be the problem today, though tiredness might prevent him from savouring to the full the lunacies of this case. It was another parallel with a Cabinet Minister's life that when a policeman needed to be at his most alert, with his judgement unimpaired, he was almost certain to have his senses blunted by fatigue.

It took the walk through St James's Park to exercise its usual magic and raise his spirits. That walk was one of the reasons why he so rarely used his official car. He found himself happily kicking the crisp leaves that lay on the path and looked around guiltily to check that no one had seen a sober-looking citizen, suddenly forgetting that his fortieth birthday was only a few years off, reverting to the habits of his youth. His eyes met those of an older man in a Crombie overcoat similarly engaged, and the conspiratorial smiles they exchanged augmented his sudden and irrational optimism.

By the time he got to the Yard he was sorting out the confused impressions of the previous day and, soon after, he was able to exude confidence in his interview with his Chief Superintendent and the Assistant Commissioner. The latter was clearly worried that he might come under pressure to put a more senior officer on the case, but Milton's emphasis on the need for tact and sensitivity in handling the Top People involved confirmed him in the job. For the time being, anyway. The only available Chief Superintendent had made his reputation as the terror of the East End gangs, and his tactics of bellowed questions and half-veiled threats, assuming that every witness he saw was a thief and a liar, were not perhaps quite what was needed for interrogating senior politicians and captains of industry.

Milton escaped to his office, relieved that he had avoided close questioning on developments in the case, and reached for the newspapers. The coverage was worse than he had feared. Only *The Times* and the *Financial Times* had thought the news of another adverse monthly trade balance sufficiently dramatic to shunt Sir Nicholas's death to the second lead story. Every single newspaper had cottoned on to the fact that the tight security in operation for the IGGY meeting made it a virtual certainty that the murderer had been among those attending it. The journalists were almost crooning over the list of those being interviewed by the police and the photographs of the most prominent IGGY attenders had all been chosen to convince the public that the country was run by thugs and psychopaths. His own photograph, snatched outside Embankment Tower, made him look like a startled mental defective—an image with which his reported comments were in keeping. On the discovery that *The Times* had indeed awarded Sir Nicholas a first-rate mind and no faults other than a somewhat acerbic wit, Milton gagged and passed on to a list of appointments the conscientious Romford had arranged for the day on his behalf. (The first four coincided with Amiss's three and a half suspects-with-a-motive.)

Nixon, Wells and Parkinson were co-dwellers in the Department of Conservation's building and were all scheduled for morning visits. Stafford could manage 2.30, and had decently offered to come to the Yard. The Plastics Extrusion Workers' leader, Alfred Shaw, had said he would be in his West End office at 4.00. There seemed little point just yet in hurrying to see the other three possibles, since no one had yet come up with any evidence that they had had any dealings with Sir Nicholas worth the name. Certainly none of them looked like a random killer. Shaw, Monday's interviews had revealed, had at least come across the Permanent Secretary at a few meetings. Milton supposed that he should see the wife and son soon to see if they had any insights into other possible motives, but that could be postponed until the chief suspects had been interviewed at greater length. More to talk to the family about, that way.

He slipped out a side door of the Yard at 9.15 for the brief walk to the department. Although preoccupied with his tactics for the morning, he found himself scrutinizing the passers-by with a view to spotting civil servants. It was all a myth about bowler hats, he realized. Their only badges of office were their brief-cases, black, with EIIR stamped on the flap. It took a few minutes of observation for him to spot that there were two classes of brief-case. The one most commonly to be seen was a limp plastic affair which clearly stamped its owner as one of the humble majority. The more exclusive kind, while much the same shape and size, was made of leather, and bulged with matters more weighty than the office-worker's proverbial sandwiches. It was rather reminiscent of the neat way in which the Chinese, to denote differences of rank while maintaining an appearance of equality, dispensed Mao-suits of rough worsted to the peasantry and of fine wool to the cadres. Apart from the brief-cases, he would have been hard put to it to see any pattern of difference between civil servants and the rest of the hurrying masses. More suits, perhaps, and those suits a little more tending towards the conservative and shabby than those of the business executives (who carried their sandwiches in slimline attaché-cases).

Milton entered the departmental building in a press of men. He must remember to ask Amiss where all the women were. Wasn't the civil service supposed to have been in the fore-front of the drive for sexual equality? On presenting his credentials to a security guard he was instructed to wait in the reception area, which offered him a collection of abstruse journals on recycling which did little to distract him from his thoughts about Harvey Nixon. Within a couple of minutes he was being led into a lift by an engaging young woman, surprisingly clad in jeans. Presumably this denoted her lowly position, or was he giving the status game too much weight now? The lift stayed empty, although there appeared to be several dozen people waiting for one, and she explained that it was exclusively for the use of those who dwelt on the top floor, where ministers and senior officials clustered together. Milton was fighting hard not to have his perceptions blurred by confused memories of all the Orwellian anti-utopias read in his late adolescence. Was the Yard more or less sinister for the uniforms seen in its corridors? Was a private lift a substitute for epaulettes and lanyards? He was led through an enormous office full of youngsters beavering away with files, staplers and an enormous photocopier, and into the inner sanctum. Milton had just enough time to observe the extreme comfort in which these ministers were housed, when he came face to face with the unfortunate Secretary of State.

My God, he thought, as Nixon produced a polite welcome and waved him to a noble leather armchair. *Does he always look like this, or is this a testimony to Sir Nicholas's efforts over the past few days? How did I miss those lines of exhaustion yesterday? And isn't his hand shaking. Play yourself in gradually, Milton.*

He spent the first ten minutes on respectful apologies for taking up time, conventional expressions of regret about this sad business and routine checking of Nixon's statement of the previous day. By then he felt that Nixon should have grasped that he was not dealing with a barbarian. Time to come to the crunch.

'It would be very helpful, sir, if you could give me your personal assessment of Sir Nicholas. It is necessary for me, you see, to get some idea of his personality if I am to come to any conclusions about why he might have been murdered.'

'Certainly, Superintendent. I worked closely with poor Sir Nicholas for almost two years, and I can say sincerely that he was a man of ability, integrity and industry. I am at a complete loss to understand why anyone would have killed him, unless of course some subversive organization wanted to embarrass the government at this critical time.'

Milton looked at him wonderingly. It would be South African agents next if he didn't get a grip on the proceedings.

'No, sir. I fear that idea is too far-fetched to be considered seriously at this stage, although I assure you that we are of course checking the backgrounds of everyone who was in Embankment Tower at that time. I regret that at present we must concentrate our attention chiefly on those who were at the ...' Milton found the word IGGY on the tip of his tongue and cursed Amiss ... 'Industry and Government Group meeting, and had the opportunity to kill Sir Nicholas.' *And that, as you all too clearly realize, includes you, sir.*

Nixon seemed to sag slightly, but he replied quietly, 'Yes, of course, Superintendent. I understand that you must do your job.'

'Can you please tell me more about your relationship with Sir Nicholas? For instance, did you like him personally?'

'Well, Superintendent, our relationship was necessarily formal, but I liked him well enough as a colleague.'

I cannot afford, thought Milton, *to let him get away with this sort of crap any longer.* He leant forward and said with a slight edge to his voice. 'Come, sir. I know we shouldn't speak ill of the dead and all that, but I know enough of what happened at yesterday's meeting to realize that Jesus Christ couldn't have *liked* Sir Nicholas if he had pulled that stunt on Him.'

Chapter Seven

He thought for a moment that Nixon was going to bluster. He sat up, squared his shoulders and looked angrily at Milton. Their eyes stayed locked for a few moments, and Milton almost hated himself for enjoying it. He didn't speak. The politician rose from his armchair and crossed the office for the cigarette box on his desk.

'Which of my loyal staff told you about that?' This with his back turned—and in a tone which strove to conceal his bitterness. Listening intently as he was, Milton felt for the first time that he'd detected a faint Lowlands lilt.

'I pieced it together from various sources,' he replied mendaciously.

'You couldn't have found out what he did except from one of my civil servants.'

'Sorry, sir? I was referring to the fact that Sir Nicholas left you in the lurch for ten minutes at a time when you needed him badly. That could not have escaped anyone present. Was there something more?'

'Oh, that,' said Nixon with relief, turning back. 'I'm sure there was a very good reason. He must have had urgent business elsewhere.' He sat down again.

'Look, sir, you've already indicated that there was more to it than that. I shall find out what it was if I have to interrogate every civil servant in the building. I have the deepest sympathy for the position in which you find yourself, but you are only going to make it worse if you don't tell me the truth about your relationship with the dead man. There must be dozens of people who know. It would come better from you.'

Face to face, Milton could see the politician at work. He was calculating his chances from every angle. After a few moments he spoke.

'Sir Nicholas was the most vicious bastard I have ever come across in thirty years in a profession which regards loyalty as weakness and decency as wetness.'

'Thank you, sir,' said Milton. *Thank you very much indeed. You're a nice bloke and I hope you didn't do it.* 'Tell me all about it.'

Nixon told him all about it, with a fluency which made Milton wonder at the standards of an organization that rated a man like this an incompetent. He seemed to forget whom he was talking to, and Milton remembered how lonely his life must be. A minister could legitimately complain to his colleagues about incompetence or obstructiveness in his Permanent Secretary, but he would make himself a laughing-stock if he complained that he was being made a fool of. With an obvious sense of relief at getting it off his chest at last, Nixon recounted a saga of endless petty humiliations. He told of the way in which Sir Nicholas made it clear, with raised eyebrow, sneer and expression of polite incredulity, that he believed his minister to be lacking in intellect, education, judgement and even political skill. 'I had no experience of office,' said Nixon miserably. 'He had thirty years' knowledge of how to play the system and was far cleverer than I was. He never did a single thing I could justifiably make a complaint about.'

Milton lost sight for a moment of his main objective in his sympathy for this poor devil. 'But surely, sir, his colleagues must have known what was going on.'

'Oh, most of it happened when there were just the two of us there. Or was done so subtly that they couldn't have been sure. The odd Deputy Secretary or Private Secretary might have had an inkling, but there was nothing they could have done about it, even if they'd been prepared to rock the boat. Personal malice or careerism would have been suspected. Sir Nicholas always took care to appear helpful in public or on paper.'

'Until yesterday.'

'Until yesterday. I really believe he must have gone mad. He didn't bother to cover his tracks. It wasn't, of course, just a matter of his leaving the room at a critical time. He set me up for a personal humiliation that could well cost me my job in the next reshuffle. "Poor chap can't cope," they'll be saying.'

Nixon went on to tell Milton of the events which had led up to the IGGY *débâcle*. His Private Secretary, thought Milton wryly, was obviously plugged as efficiently into the network as was Amiss. Nixon knew the whole story.

'You didn't know all this until you came back here yesterday afternoon and made enquiries?'

'No, but I was pretty sure that he was responsible at least for the speech which I was given to deliver. An ego like his could never resist putting something of itself into a draft speech, even in those circumstances. Beautifully done, of course, rubbish though it was. And when the threatened attack from the TUC which had ostensibly necessitated my presence didn't materialize, I had no doubt about who had invented it. I've been honest with you, Superintendent. I had every reason to kill the swine yesterday morning. I also had the opportunity, apparently. But I didn't do it. Oddly enough I was almost grateful to him for bringing the whole business to a head. He had given me a reasonable chance of being able to nail him at last, and he had made me realize once and for all that I was happier as an M.P. than as a minister and the sooner I returned to the back-benches the better.'

'I am extremely grateful to you, sir. I assure you that I shan't abuse your confidence.'

Nixon got to his feet and held out his hand. 'I apologize for being so evasive at the beginning, Superintendent. Answering straight questions doesn't come easily to a politician.'

As Milton closed the door behind him he caught himself wishing that he had Nixon as a constituency M.P. rather than the smooth, intensely able, totally inhuman rising star who presently graced the position. He doubted if he would feel the same way about the man he was to meet next.

Chapter Eight

That Milton was already late for his appointment with Wells was made clear to him by the way in which he was greeted by one of the two minions inhabiting Wells's modest outer office. The girl seemed slightly agitated and fussed about how busy the minister was. *But isn't he called a PUSS?* thought Milton, confused again. Then he realized that this would hardly be a respectful term of verbal address. Equally, you could hardly go about calling people 'Parliamentary Under-Secretary of State' if you ever wanted to get any business done. Presumably 'minister' was a catch-all title of respect for any politician holding even the most lowly of offices in the government. He was grateful he could stick to 'sir'.

The girl had said that Wells was in the middle of an important phone call. Her insistence that it couldn't be interrupted was so intense that it seemed that the fate of the government must rest on its successful conclusion. Milton wondered if she were an idiot, but, while he waited, his close observation showed her colleague to bear equal signs of strain. In view of what Amiss had told him, he guessed that their master's self-importance and ambition made him a nightmare to work for.

Initially he felt ashamed of his unprofessional prejudice when Wells welcomed him with affability and charm, ushered him into his office and urged him towards the most comfortable chair (altogether less commodious than Nixon's). However, a couple of brief exchanges overheard from the outer office, whither Wells had dashed with a last-minute instruction once Milton was seated, confirmed his original suspicions. Amiss was right. The man was clearly a Grade A shit. That was a relief. He couldn't afford to like another of his prime suspects.

Milton went through the same rigmarole he had gone through in the first ten minutes with Nixon, though in this case there seemed to be no need to calm the man's nerves. Wells was relaxed. Milton sensed that he was trying to hide his amusement at the inability of the clod-hopping detective to get his evidence straight the first time round. Anyway, Wells's account of his movements over Monday lunch-time had been correctly noted and typed up. So far so good. *Come on, smirk so I can see it, and we'll have the gloves off.* Wells looked more serious when Milton asked about his relationship with Sir Nicholas.

'I can't say it was particularly good, Superintendent. You know what civil servants are like. They want it all their own way and are absolutely determined to reject new ideas. I see my job as helping to ensure that the radical commitments on which we were elected are put into force—and quickly—but these damned bureaucrats never lose an opportunity to put a spoke in the wheels. I'm not the sort of person to lie down under this treatment, so I suppose my blunt criticisms are the reason why my relations with some of the officials—including Sir Nicholas—have often been rather strained.'

'Are you saying that you got on no better or worse with Sir Nicholas than with many of his colleagues?'

Wells paused for a moment. *He's too fly a bugger not to realize that I can check up on this.*

'Well, to be quite frank, I should say that I normally got on worse with Sir Nicholas than with any of the others. Even by their standards he was exceptionally arrogant and unhelpful. He was forever accusing me of being irresponsible in trying to bring important information to the attention of the public. He didn't seem to understand that one needs to expose injustice if one is to remedy it. I see my job as a ...'

Aware that once in his stride Wells was likely to go on all day, Milton interrupted.

'Did you feel personal dislike for each other?'

'I can't answer for him, though I expect he would dislike anyone who stood up to him. I wouldn't demean myself by feeling dislike for a man who merely symbolized the inadequacy of the way in which we allow an unelected executive to undermine the democracy of this country. I didn't look upon him as an individual, so much as an example of what I have set out to curb.'

Milton felt tired. Did the fellow ever talk in anything other than political clichés?

'Was he disliked as an individual by anybody, to your knowledge, sir?'

'How would I know?'

Milton realized that Wells was telling the truth. His kind simply wasn't interested in personal relationships. He would never speculate about who felt what about whom and why. He probably never listened to gossip unless he felt it politically necessary. People who believed in conspiracies were always like that. Individuals were to them symbols or tools, depending on their position. And he was far too self-satisfied to be vulnerable to the kind of weapons which Sir Nicholas had used on poor old Harvey Nixon.

'Well, sir, can I ask you to tell me about the events leading up to the meeting of the Industry and Government Group yesterday? I understand you were originally to be the department's representative?'

'I certainly was. And I may tell you, Superintendent, that I was furious when I arrived and found that I had been replaced. I had put a great deal of work into mastering that subject—which is one of the greatest importance for this department and the paper industry of this country. I made those damned officials work hard for a change on the speech I was to make there. And even then I had to rewrite it myself. Civil servants. They have absolutely no political sense …'

'You arrived at the meeting still expecting to speak, sir?'

'Certainly, I did. And then found myself hustled to one side and prevented from making any contribution to a discussion on a subject about which, I may tell you, I knew far more than anyone else present.'

'Didn't you find it very odd that you hadn't been informed that Mr Nixon was to replace you, sir?'

'Well, naturally I put it down to some bloody civil-service cock-up.'

'Are you saying that Sir Nicholas, whom I understand knew about this change of plan on Friday, failed to perform the simple courtesy of letting you know about it?'

'Oh, I don't know. It doesn't matter now anyway.'

'It matters to me, sir. Any of Sir Nicholas's actions or inactions over the last few days may have some bearing on this case. If he was failing to perform his duties it may have implications that we can't know about at this stage. You must know whether he got, or tried to get, in touch with you before the meeting.'

Got you, you bastard, crowed Milton to himself as he watched the indecision on Wells's face.

'Well, yes. I gather he made some effort to get in touch with me.'

'When, sir?'

'On Friday.'

'What exactly did he do, sir?'

'He rang my home after I had left the office.'

'And did he speak to anyone, sir?'

'To my wife.'

God, thought Milton. *This is like drawing teeth.*

'And what did he say?'

'Merely that he wanted to speak to me.'

'Didn't she tell you, sir?'

'Well, she couldn't, actually. I was away for the weekend and she couldn't get in touch with me.'

'Did she comment on Sir Nicholas's manner at all?'

'No, she didn't. It seems to me that you are making a great deal out of nothing here. Couldn't you be spending your time more productively with some of the other people who were at the meeting? Whether Sir Nicholas spoke politely to my wife during a perfectly mundane telephone call three days before he was murdered can hardly have any bearing on the case.'

Milton studied Wells's face. The small blue eyes stared back at him defiantly. He was pleased to see how the affability had given way to irritation. Time for a kidney punch.

'Anything might have a bearing on the case, sir. Sir Nicholas's state of mind is of great interest to me. I think I had better have a word with your wife about the telephone call. She might be able to give me some of the flavour of it. Could you please give me her address and telephone number?'

He watched the look of calculation reappear. The chances were good that Wells hadn't been able to repair relations with his wife sufficiently to guarantee her keeping her mouth shut about his weekend.

'Her address, sir?'

'Oh, there's no need for that, Superintendent,' replied Wells crossly. 'I'll tell you about it. I object on principle to having my private life interfered with, but I suppose I can't stop you. By sheer ill-luck Sir Nicholas gave my wife some information which seriously upset her—namely that I wasn't, as she supposed, away at a departmental conference.'

'Where were you, sir?'

'In the flat of a female friend of mine in north London.'

'So your wife concluded you had been deceiving her, sir?'

'Yes.'

'And when did she let you know this?'

Wells hesitated for a moment, and caved in. 'When I rang her just before the meeting yesterday morning.'

'She must have been very upset.'

'She was.'

'So must you, sir. Particularly with Sir Nicholas.'

'Yes, damn it, I was. My wife gave me the impression that Sir Nicholas had raised her suspicions deliberately.'

'Thank you, sir. I think that's all I need to know.'

'Now, listen, Superintendent. You're not to run away with the lunatic idea that I killed Sir Nicholas because he had exposed my affair to my wife. She'll come round. Women always do if you make enough fuss of them. She must realize that a man in my position has lots of temptations and needs to relax occasionally. I can't spend every free weekend with squalling children.'

Milton rose and looked down at Wells. 'The police do not go in for lunatic ideas, sir. I have already established that you were one of those with the opportunity to murder Sir Nicholas. I have now discovered that you had a motive. I will come to no conclusions until I have discovered how many others are similarly placed.'

He looked back as he made his exit and had the satisfaction of seeing Wells sitting with his head in his hands. The girl in the outer office reacted uncertainly to the happy smile he flashed at her.

Chapter Nine

As Milton headed towards Parkinson's room he was hailed by the be-jeaned girl from Nixon's office with a message asking him to ring Romford urgently. She showed him to a private telephone and within seconds he was connected to an agitated sergeant.

'There's a new development, sir. A postcard has arrived addressed to the Commissioner which simply says "What about Lady Clark and Martin Jenkins?"'

'Jesus!'

'Of course, sir, it may be just a bit of unfounded malice.'

Milton suppressed the urge to scream at Romford for his uncanny ability to state the obvious. 'Yes, but we'll have to follow it up,' he said, stating the no less obvious. 'What does the postmark tell us?'

'Westminster area. Seven-thirty yesterday evening.'

'Anything special about the card? Handwriting?'

'It was in an envelope, sir. Handprinted in block capitals. The card's one of those saucy seaside ones. About some bloke whose missus is having it off with the coalman. She's got these black handprints on her ...'

'Look, I can't do anything until I've seen the rest of the people on today's list, but try to make appointments for me to see Lady Clark and Jenkins—separately, of course—later this evening or early tomorrow morning. Make the usual noises about it's being simply a matter of routine. I'll see you when I get back just before two.'

He rang off, irritated that he must immediately see Parkinson without having any time to reflect on the implications of this piece of news. His overwhelming feeling was one of injustice at fate's determination to go on finding new motives. As he hurried towards Parkinson's rather cramped little room, he found he was intensely curious about him. Nixon had had the Sir Nicholas treatment for only two years. Parkinson had apparently had it for about eight, and should therefore be showing signs of premature and bitter old age. Try as he might, he could conjure up no memory of him from their hurried meeting the previous day.

He was rather taken aback by the relaxed and courteous man who unwound his lanky form from his chair and shook hands with an easy and sympathetic greeting.

'This must be rather hellish for you, Superintendent. It can't be easy finding anything out from such glib individuals as all of us suspects must be.'

Milton was so taken aback by this expression of human sympathy—and the ready acceptance of suspicion—that it took him a minute to get rolling with his routine lead-in. He was so familiar with it by now that he could virtually switch off his brain as Parkinson helpfully made the appropriate replies, and he was able to observe his companion with more attention than he had initially been able to give to Nixon or Wells. He was particularly struck by Parkinson's extraordinarily handsome face. He had the high cheekbones and keen eyes of a scientist in a romantic novel. Milton found it incredible that anyone who looked like that, had such an agreeable manner, and was, in addition, a highly intelligent man, could have been held back from promotion by even a first-rate machinator. He felt a grudging respect for Sir Nicholas. At least he had set himself one real challenge.

He pulled himself together to hear his voice going on to the question about personal relationships.

'I resented Nicholas,' said Parkinson, 'and he seemed to hate me, but I never managed to work out why. Until about eight years ago I thought of him as a good and amusing friend. I doubt if any people who got to know him well in recent years would believe that, but he could in the early days be a perceptive and sympathetic confidant.'

'Things changed?'

'With a vengeance, Superintendent, if that's the right word. I was, I admit, shattered by the alteration in my old friend once I began to work for him. You should know that I used to be a scientist and came late to administration.'

Milton wondered if he was imagining the bitter edge in Parkinson's voice.

'It was Nicholas who first persuaded me to come into the scientific civil service, as it was he who later persuaded me that I could make a better contribution in a wider context—and incidentally a brilliant career—if I switched to the administrative class. I was delighted to find that he would be my first boss. For the first few months I tried to explain away his unhelpfulness and lack of sympathy with my inevitable ignorance, and to interpret his taste for showing me up in front of colleagues as an over-enthusiastic attempt to show that he would not let our friendship affect his judgement.'

'But you didn't convince yourself for long?'

'No. It rapidly became unarguable that he was deliberately setting out to damage me.'

'Why did you put up with it, sir? Couldn't you have transferred to a different post or even left the civil service altogether?'

'I couldn't find the grounds for a transfer. No one would have wanted me until I had some worthwhile experience. Anyway, I'm naturally obstinate and I wouldn't give up. I was determined to show that I could do anything I turned my hand to. I couldn't believe that anything Nicholas could do would hide my virtues from my other colleagues. Call it arrogance, if you like, but I wasn't used to failing.'

'And did you succeed?'

'You know I didn't. Even one morning in a civil-service building must have shown you that a man's success can be measured by the size of his room, the quality of the furniture and the number of staff in his outer office. I have exactly the same status as I had eight years ago and I owe it all to my old friend.'

Milton was feeling taken aback by all this frankness. He wasn't going to need any of his inside knowledge for this one.

'I stuck it out for the two years I worked directly for Nicholas, and with his elevation to Deputy Secretary I breathed a sigh of relief and began to look forward to happier days. I was a fool. I got a new Under Secretary—a most fair-minded man—who thought highly of me and told me so, but he didn't have the clout to dissipate the view of me which had gone round the department. I don't know if it's the same in your profession, Superintendent, but certainly here, once those who don't know much about you have heard that you are superficially bright but have no depth, they write you off without even thinking about it as a "fly-weight", or a "good front man". Any mistakes made in your area are your fault. Any triumphs are due to some clever young member of your staff. By the time I realized that this was the way things were inevitably going I had left it too late to be employable again as a scientist. All I could do was to take whatever job was offered me, do the best I could and hope that someone, somewhere, would recognize my worth. Nobody did. You see, I had no old-boy network. I had come into the service years after my contemporaries and no one had got to know me before Nicholas's assessment of me got about.'

'You mean you hadn't the faintest chance of promotion?'

'I wouldn't say that. I felt—and feel—reasonably confident that they'll give me one step up before I retire. Even fly-weights get to be Under Secretaries. But that'll be all. Even Nicholas's death is unlikely to change things much. Certainly not enough to have made it worthwhile murdering him.'

'It would certainly seem, sir, that if you were going to murder him you left it a bit late in the day.'

'Precisely, Superintendent. It's been going on so long that I've had to come to terms with it. I now take a minimalist view of my work. I do as much as I think is required to keep me in line for promotion, but no more. I delegate a good deal. I enjoy my life outside: my golf handicap is down to six; I see a great deal of my wife, children and friends—and there aren't many senior civil servants who can boast of that.'

'Nor many senior policemen, sir,' said Milton morosely.

Parkinson laughed. 'You should try it, Superintendent. It's surprisingly enjoyable. I feel compassion but little sympathy at the fretting and panic my colleagues indulge in every time there is some hiccup. They even talk about their families sometimes as if they are a sort of extra burden placed on them by politicians.'

'So you had no reason to be particularly angry with Sir Nicholas yesterday morning?'

'No, I had no more reason to dislike him than I'd always had, although I felt a considerable distaste for the way in which he landed our unfortunate Secretary of State in the lurch. No doubt you've heard about that.'

'I have, sir. And I gather you weren't able to do anything to help Mr Nixon.'

'No. I have never had anything to do with paper recycling. It was silly to have me there, but for some reason the appropriate people couldn't make it. Not that there was any need for them to attend. It was an area of special interest to Nicholas. No one was a better choice to be at the minister's hand. God knows what he thought he was doing leaving like that. I tried to take the charitable view that he had a stomach cramp or something.'

'Well, sir. I am extremely grateful to you for being so frank with me. I must be getting on now. I have several more inter-views ahead of me.'

'Goodbye. And remember, take up golf. It alters your perspec-tive. Or are you anxious to be a Chief Superintendent?'

'I'll be lucky to stay a superintendent if I don't get this case sorted out soon,' said Milton and they exchanged smiles of understanding as he hurried off to find some lunch.

Chapter Ten

Amiss had felt light-headed as he walked into his office shortly after 9.00 that morning. He put it down to lack of sleep, excitement and a glorious sense of freedom from the demands of Sir Nicholas. Working for Douglas Sanders was going to be a doddle. It wasn't just that he would be pleasant to his Private Secretary; he was known to be considerate about all his personal staff. Amiss looked forward to a future in which the office would run smoothly without his having to cajole, charm, inject team spirit and rally the troops ceaselessly to forestall the riot he always feared on the days when Sir Nicholas was in an offensive (bad) rather than distant (par) or patronizing (good) mood. They would even be able to get rid of the Greek typeface which Sir Nicholas had demanded for the golfball machine. Amiss had often wondered if the sod deliberately inserted Greek words into almost everything he wrote primarily because he knew they would annoy the recipients or because he took pleasure in the knowledge that they compelled Julia to change the golfball several times in the course of typing even one page. Amiss shuddered at the recollection of the rows that used to ensue every time Julia got a letter wrong. Nothing snapped Sir Nicholas's cobweb-like patience so quickly as a misplaced omega. He could hear running through his memory the thrice-weekly tirade about cretins, universal illiteracy and typists who couldn't read, let alone type.

Only Julia was in the office, and Amiss could see that she was in good spirits. There was no crap about that kid. She wouldn't pretend to be sorry about Sir Nicholas. She had already gone home on the previous evening by the time Amiss had got back to the office, so she was all set for a pleasurable chat about the good news. Her first words didn't disappoint.

'The old bastard had it coming. Any idea who did it? I'd like to get up a collection for him.'

'You can put me down for a fiver.'

'So it wasn't you, was it? No. I suppose if you were ever going to do it, you'd have done it the time he made you cancel your holiday to go with him on that tour of Glasgow recycling works.'

They fell to discussing the details of the murder, and Julia sighed contentedly as Amiss rehashed the details which had appeared in his morning newspaper.

'I'm only sorry it was so quick. I'd have preferred him to die of slow poisoning.'

'Ssshh,' hissed Amiss warningly, as Gladys came stumbling in, plastic bags crammed with provisions from the supermarket, destined for reprocessing that evening into a meal for her unpleasant husband. Nose dripping, tightly belted coat setting off her thick hips and covering only partially the uneven crimplene hemline of her most unattractive dress, apologies and complaints tumbling from her in confused and overlapping sentences which betrayed not the slightest connection between brain and mouth (unless it was, as Sir Nicholas had been wont to point out—usually to her—that there was none of the former to be connected to the latter), Gladys was ready to give her best in the service of Her Majesty's Government.

Amiss gave her his commiserating look—for Gladys's lot was too miserable at work or home to make encouragement more than an insult—and watched her absently as she divested herself of her top coverings, lamented over the torn lining, dropped one bag of shopping with cries of alarm, knocked her leg painfully on the corner of her desk, and settled down ready for her daily work of making a hash of the appointments diary and the log-

ging of the endless flow of papers. It was Gladys's malign fate
to have been landed in the most fraught office in the building
while being wholly unable to cope with its demands.

Amazing as it seemed, she hadn't heard the news. She had
had Monday afternoon off to wait for the gasman—who, of
course (Gladys's ill-luck being constant), hadn't turned up. And
Gladys never listened to or read the news. She watched seamy
soap operas and read romantic novels as an antidote to the dreary
awfulness of her life. It took several minutes before he and Julia
could stop her disjointed wails about the gas board and get the
story of the murder through to her.

Gladys went faint and had to be revived with a cup of coffee.
Amiss felt he couldn't stand it any more when she began to produce pious sentiments about the tragedy of it all and the blow
it must be to his poor wife and son. If anyone should have been
dancing on Sir Nicholas's grave it was Lady Clark, but then,
Amiss supposed, anyone who could be fond of a husband like
hers was hardly likely to be a harsh critic. When she started on
the generosity of Sir Nicholas in giving her a box of chocolates
the previous Christmas, Amiss decided it was time to leave before
a second murder was done.

'Look after Gladys, Julia,' he said. 'Sanders won't be moving
up here until this afternoon, so I'll have to go down and spend
a few hours in his office this morning. Ask George to stand in
for me when he gets in.'

'What about a drink at lunchtime?' asked Julia. 'Seems to
me we've got something to celebrate.'

'Shut up,' hissed Amiss savagely, fearful of the effect of such
heartlessness on Gladys. But there was no danger there. Gladys
was still maundering on about 'cut off in his prime'. 'Why not?
We've all had a shock and a communal drink will help to steady
our nerves. Have the office manned on a rota system. See you
in the Cardinal at 1.00.'

He picked up a batch of papers and escaped.

Chapter Eleven

He found himself a spare desk in Sander's outer office and dealt with the urgent paper work. Sanders called him in at 10.30 to take notes at the regular Tuesday morning Deputy Secretaries' meeting, which he was now chairing in place of Sir Nicholas. There were perfunctory expressions of shock and regret from the four Dep. Secs present. They were all too intelligent to put up more than an adequate pretence of being personally bereaved, but they certainly weren't going to let their hair down in front of a junior colleague. (That they might do later—probably seeking each other out individually on pretexts and settling down to a series of cosy reminiscences. In all likelihood, there would be an informal competition to compose the best barbed epitaph.)

It was a relaxed and pleasant hour. Sanders was helpful, constructive, and understanding about the problems caused by new legislation, under-staffing and all those other obstacles to achievement which Sir Nicholas had always discounted as feeble excuses. Only last week there had been a fraught ten minutes over the brief which Blows had sent in on a Monday morning, apparently the work of a palsied typewriter afflicted with quavering capitals and sticking letters. Sir Nicholas had held it up between finger and thumb and had ignored the information that Blows had had to write it—and type it with two fingers—over the weekend. He had almost succeeded in making the serene and accomplished Miss Beckett lose her temper by his open contempt for her wetness in allowing her subordinates to produce such messy work, garnished with the implication that as a woman she should at least be capable of overseeing the typing. It had been one of those meetings which left Sir Nicholas in excellent spirits and his colleagues sick with fury. None of that with Sanders, Amiss was happy to note. This *was* going to be a doddle.

Amiss was back at his desk shortly after 11.30, ready to get down to what he had already decided was his main business of the day. If he was going to be a grass, he might as well be a super-grass.

His first phone call, on a trumped-up excuse, was to a chatty man in the plastics recycling division. It was easy enough to manoeuvre Latham into talking about the people he knew who had been at the IGGY meeting. Latham had nothing to add to what Amiss already knew about Archibald Stafford, but he also knew Alfred Shaw pretty well. Amiss was thankful that he didn't need to appear inquisitive. Latham loved gossiping too much to need prompting.

'… so I don't suppose Alf will be too sorry about what's happened. There was no love lost between him and Clark.'

'But they didn't know each other well, did they?'

'No. It was just Clark's habit of calling him "Alf"—and sometimes "Sid"—in that sneery way he had when he found himself in company with those he deemed proles. Otherwise it was just a matter of the odd clash at meetings. We kept Alf away from Clark as much as possible, and he was quite happy dealing with us instead.'

That would be good news for Milton tonight, thought Amiss as he put the phone down. He wouldn't want more motives. His next call—to the Private Secretary to Gerald Hunter, Secretary of State for Energy—was also encouragingly negative. It was obvious that Hunter would have had difficulty in recognizing Sir Nicholas if he met him in the street. Amiss couldn't think of anyone who could tell him anything about Norman Grewe, Chairman of Industrial Electronics Ltd, but he was pretty sure he could be ruled out. He couldn't think of any occasion other than the odd formal business dinner where they could have met.

Grewe was a recent recruit to IGGY and wouldn't have seen Sir Nicholas there more than twice.

Amiss decided to give up on Grewe. He had only one suspect left to investigate—Martin Jenkins, the President of the Fitters' Union. He doubted if there would be anything positive here either. Clark wouldn't have any dealings with Jenkins in the normal course of events. Amiss had had to give a lot of thought to fabricating an adequate excuse to ring the department's trades union adviser, but it was a risk worth taking. Cronin was as gregarious and gossipy as Latham and liked nothing better than passing on discreditable bits of information about those people on whom he fawned professionally.

Cronin was in. That was a piece of luck. He spent most of his time hanging round trades union headquarters looking for juicy bits of scandal (and useful birds to pull. Eligible bachelor—he had no trouble. He was even a challenge—at the first dinner together, she always heard how his heart was broken ten years ago and he could never love again. That also provided a useful get-out when a more tempting prospect came in sight. The place was littered with women who had succumbed. This was his idea of keeping in touch with the grass roots.). He was delighted to hear from Amiss—so delighted that there was no danger of his doubting his reason for ringing up. They got the pretext over with quickly—Cronin giving Amiss the figure that was already staring up at him from a memorandum on his desk. Amiss fed him a few harmless bits of inside information on the happenings of the previous day, and the conversation came round to the trades unionists present.

'At least they'll be in the clear,' he said. 'Sir Nicholas never had much time for them.'

'I'm not so sure of that,' said a gleeful voice. 'It'll be fun if the police get to know about Jenkins and Sir Nicholas's missus.'

'What?' yelled Amiss, temporarily off his guard.

'Didn't you know? It's been the talk of the Fitters' headquarters for ages. A life-long socialist bachelor falling for a classy piece like that? Dynamite.'

Amiss knew perfectly well that Cronin was capable of making a scandal out of the sight of two people chatting at a dinner party, so he couldn't take this at face value.

'You're having me on.'

Cronin was piqued.

'I am not. They've been seen lunching together several times and Jenkins's secretary says they're always ringing each other up.'

'Well, stone the crows!' Amiss doubted no longer. Cronin's way with secretaries was legendary. He knew that the hand that controls the telephone has access to one hell of a lot of gossip. It was amazing how pathetically people trusted their secretaries. There were very few invulnerable to Cronin's seedy charm, and the drinks he lavished on any likely source.

'I suppose the police will get onto it eventually,' said Cronin hopefully.

Yes, you shit, thought Amiss. *There's nothing you'd like better than seeing your avowed friend Jenkins embarrassed.*

'I wouldn't count on it,' he said. 'They didn't look to me as if they had much of a clue about anything. But then, I only saw them for a few minutes. They may have TUC moles for all I know. Anyway, thanks for your help with the Extrusion stats. I knew you'd be able to help. See you.'

Amiss wondered if Cronin would ensure that the Yard got to know about Jenkins and Lady Clark and concluded that he wouldn't. He would be too terrified of being spotted as the source and having his access to future scandal jeopardized. Did this come under the heading of urgent information of the kind Milton would need immediately? He thought so. The negative report on Alf Shaw could wait until the evening, but he'd better get a message about Jenkins through to Milton by the channels they had set up on their way to the tube the previous night.

He couldn't get away without a chat with one of Sanders's staff, so it was almost 1.00—time for him to be off to the Cardinal— when he finally found an empty room with a telephone. He dialled the number he had been given and asked for Mrs Milton.

Tuesday Afternoon

Chapter Twelve

Milton had grabbed a hasty lunch in a pub frequented by civil servants from neighbouring offices. He found himself compulsively eavesdropping on their chat about work and people—especially once he had overheard several disparaging references to Sir Nicholas. He had time for quiet reflection only on his walk back to the Yard, and during that time he concluded that the postcard was probably a hoax. After all, the Yard received dozens of anonymous missives every day accusing anyone of anything. It would be credulous to believe this one. Still, he would have to go through the motions with Lady Clark and Martin Jenkins, though he would have to go very carefully. They would have every right to lodge an official complaint if they were interrogated closely on their private lives on the strength of an unsubstantiated allegation. Milton knew Jenkins's reputation as a hard man, and Lady Clark would have the protection of her new status as grief-stricken widow.

It was ten to two when he reached his office. Romford was waiting with details of new appointments he had made and confirmation of double- and treble-checked alibis; the list of possible murderers from IGGY still remained at eight. He had a message asking Milton to ring his wife urgently at a Soho restaurant. Knowing that when Ann said urgent she meant urgent, Milton told Romford to hold Archibald Stafford for a few minutes and rang the restaurant. Fortunately the staff knew

Ann well. She did most of her business entertaining there. She was on within a minute.

'Darling, your young man has been on to me already. He rang just before one. I liked him. He identified himself as Deep Throat.'

'What did he say?' asked Milton.

'Just "Tell Jim the word is that Jenkins and Lady C. have been having it off."'

Milton thanked Ann and rang off. Since he couldn't admit to a source, he wouldn't be able to use this information directly, but it would certainly make him easier in his mind while taking the necessary risks with the errant pair. He sighed. He didn't really enjoy playing the heavy policeman, especially when it involved prying into intimate relationships. Still, he wasn't being paid to have finer feelings. He would harden his heart before he saw Lady Clark at six. Now he had better focus on Archibald Stafford and his imminent departure from the Plastics Conversion Company.

Stafford was every envious little person's idea of a prosperous man. From his hand-made shoes to his elegant hair he was spotless, faultlessly groomed and sweet-smelling—Colour-Supplement Man made flesh. He carried a hand-tooled leather executive case with brass trimmings, and Milton made a private bet with himself that his car boasted a television set and a cocktail cabinet. He tried not to dislike him.

It wasn't too hard. The first few routine minutes showed Stafford to be quite simply a nice man. Milton thought that he probably dressed like a prat because he thought it necessary to impress. There wasn't any difficulty in getting the story of the government grant out of him. It was just a matter of well-placed questions about his professional relations with Sir Nicholas and the closeness of the links between his company and the department.

Not that this frankness meant anything, necessarily. Stafford might be nice, but he was clearly sensible as well, and had no reason to doubt that the police would hear about the circumstances of the grant from some civil servant or other. He didn't, of course, know what Amiss had known about the importance of Sir Nicholas's role in the affair, but he admitted his suspicions.

'I did wonder, Superintendent, if Nicholas had been entirely frank with me. He assured me frequently that he was taking a personal interest in getting the grant approved, yet he never gave me any word of warning of what was going to happen. If I had had any foreknowledge I could have made a proper case for myself. I had been concentrating on making a case for the company.'

'Did you tax him with this?'

'I rang him at the weekend and asked him why he had said nothing. He was very stiff. Talked about departmental confidentiality and made me feel as if I had been improperly trying to pull strings. That was a distortion and I felt very sore about it. I never tried to misuse my friendship with Nicholas. He claimed to have a high opinion of my managerial talents and I reasonably assumed that he would pass this on.'

'Did you have a row?'

'Nicholas wasn't the sort of man you could have a real row with. He just went stiffer and stiffer and more and more pompous and ended the conversation by saying he wished to express his regrets at my misfortune and hoped that when I had had time to get over it we could have lunch again.'

Milton wondered if this was true. Knowing the state of mind Sir Nicholas had been in over the weekend he could well have been intensely insulting to Stafford. He might even have made it clear that he had been instrumental in getting the offensive conditions attached to the offer. However, there was no way of checking up on this now. Perhaps Lady Clark might know something about the phone call. Nothing more to learn here.

Milton had just thanked Stafford and said goodbye when Romford dashed in unceremoniously with the news of the second murder.

Chapter Thirteen

The rather muted celebrations of Sir Nicholas's staff were over by 2.30. They were necessarily muted because even Julia realized that there were limits to bad taste. After she had left just before 2.00 to relieve Gladys, who was manning the office alone, the conversation flagged and finally died. Amiss was too preoccupied with his private thoughts to inject any life into the proceedings, and at 2.30 he realized with a start that he had better be getting back to the office, as Sanders was due to move into Sir Nicholas's room at 3.00 and it was up to him to remove in advance any of the late unlamented's private belongings.

'Shouldn't we wait for Gladys?' asked George.

'Give her another ten minutes, but the poor old bat has probably gone shopping instead. You know she doesn't really like coming to the pub.'

He walked back hurriedly, arriving to find Julia sitting comfortably in his chair painting her nails.

'Nothing urgent?'

'Not a thing. It's been as quiet as the grave,' and Julia began to laugh immoderately at her own wit.

'Gladys didn't turn up.'

'Well, I don't know where she went. She wasn't here when I got back.'

'That's not like her,' said Amiss, frowning. 'I wonder if she felt ill and went home. But she'd have left a note.'

'Oh, she probably thought it was O.K. to pop out shopping since everything was so quiet. You know she can't resist the market at lunch-time.'

'Come and give me a hand loading up Sir Nicholas's belongings then, Julia—if your nail varnish will permit.'

'It's all been done, Robert. His wife and son came in just before I left and they seem to have cleared the lot.'

'Lord, I should have been here to meet them.'

'Well, we couldn't find you so I did the honours. They didn't seem to be in a chatty mood anyway.'

Amiss looked into the inner office and saw that indeed a clean sweep of intimate objects had been made. The desk and tables no longer displayed Sir Nicholas's few ascetic *objets d'art*, and his pictures had gone as well. He debated whether to clear the drawers and small filing-cabinet, but decided against it. There would be very little of a personal nature there and Sanders had better be left to decide what he wanted to keep and what should be chucked out.

'Mind you,' said Julia, 'I'm a bit surprised Gladys didn't make it to the pub. She was dying to tell you about yesterday morning.'

'What about yesterday morning?'

'Her seeing Sir Nicholas after the IGGY meeting.'

'What? She didn't mention that this morning.'

'You didn't stay round long enough to hear. She remembered it with a shriek about half an hour after you left. You know how muddled she gets. It took that long for her to get the details straight and realize that she must have been one of the last to see him.'

'Has she told the police?'

'I told her she should, but she said she was that upset she wouldn't do anything about it till after lunch. She's probably trying to work up her courage with a quick rummage through the clothes racks. She'll be O.K. when she gets back. Still, God help the policeman who tries to get any sense out of her.'

'How did she come to see Sir Nicholas, anyway?'

'Miss Beckett sent her over to get his signature on something urgent. She told her to hang around and wait until the meeting was over.'

'But you must have known she had gone there. Why didn't you say so earlier?'

'I didn't know,' said Julia in a wounded tone. 'I wasn't in the room when she was sent and she buggered off home afterwards, didn't she? Gasman, remember?'

Amiss was opening his mouth to ask why one of the others hadn't said something, when caution prevailed. He couldn't afford to look too interested in the investigation. Besides, just because he was involved in trying to nab the murderer didn't mean that anyone else's minds would be running along the same track. To Julia, George and Bernard the death of Sir Nicholas was a drama, but they weren't much interested in the details of the case. They were just enjoying speculating about how much fun it would be if the murderer turned out to be someone they knew. The Secretary of State, for instance. Or himself. They'd be able to dine out on that for weeks.

George and Bernard shambled back a couple of minutes later. Amiss wondered if he could trust them to give Sanders a proper welcome if he slipped out and phoned Mrs Milton again. No, he was being unnecessarily fussy. The news about Gladys could keep till she got back. But why wasn't she back? Surely to God nothing could have happened to her? Christ, supposing she had seen something yesterday morning? Odds against, surely. Anyway, he couldn't do anything now, as Sanders was just coming into the room.

Amiss and Sanders spent a pleasant half-hour talking over current work and organizing the next few days. Sir Nicholas wasn't mentioned. Amiss wondered if Sanders knew about the events at the IGGY meeting and decided it wasn't his job to tell him. The Secretary of State could fill him in if he wanted to. Or if he didn't, Parkinson could. For Amiss to bring the matter up would smack of disloyalty to his old master, and, prick though Sanders undoubtedly knew his predecessor to be, etiquette prevented any additional evidence of his misdemeanours being provided by his Private Secretary. Amiss tried to imagine the civil service without its etiquette—staffed by straightforward people who always spoke their minds. He couldn't. You'd have to throw out the whole workforce and start again from the beginning.

'I must confess to having cast covetous eyes on this room over the past few years,' said Sanders. 'It must have the best view in Whitehall.' Leaving his chair, he walked across the room to the window, from which you could see as far as the City and beyond. 'I hated my room, you know. The only things I could see from there were the windows of neighbouring sky-scrapers, and just enough of Big Ben to be tantalizing.'

He surveyed the scene with contentment. 'I always liken it to ... Jesus Christ!'

Elderly civil servants didn't blaspheme. A sick feeling overcame Amiss as he hurried to where Sanders was pointing. 'Oh, no. Oh Jesus, no.'

There couldn't be any doubt about whose was the body lying behind the sofa. Even though Gladys was lying on her face, her shabby coat, scuffed shoes and laddered stockings were unmistakeable. And in a wave of nausea he recognized also the knife which was sticking out of her back as one of her favourite possessions, an elaborately wrought paper-knife he had brought her back from a recent holiday in North Africa.

Neither of them made any move towards the body. It had a very dead look. Sanders recovered himself first.

'Who is it?' he asked. 'Gladys?' Her shabbiness was so highly developed that even a slight acquaintanceship made her memorable.

'Yes.'

'She didn't deserve this,' said Sanders. 'Nicholas did, but Gladys didn't.'

'You can say that again,' said Amiss in a thick voice, as he stumbled over to the desk to phone the police.

Chapter Fourteen

Milton was along within ten minutes, accompanied by Sergeants Pike and Romford and a police doctor. Amiss sat in his office trying to recover and calm Julia, who was blaming herself for having left Gladys alone in the office.

'You mustn't think like that,' he said miserably, trying in turn not to blame himself for not staying long enough with her that morning to find out what she'd seen. He would have been able to bundle her off to the police immediately and she'd have been safe.

It took a long time to comfort Julia. Tough-minded she might be, but however much Gladys had got on her nerves, she had been fond of her. Julia kept echoing Sander's unexpected words. 'She didn't deserve it. She didn't deserve it. He did.'

Amiss eventually turned Julia over to George and retreated to his own desk with his own black thoughts. It seemed like hours before the police doctor had finished, the stretcher carried away and Milton and his sergeants left in possession of the inner office, which Sanders had thankfully yielded up. The police doctor had put the time of death at between 1.00 and 1.30, so the main job was once again the mechanical checking of alibis.

Milton decided that for the moment he couldn't entertain the possibility that Gladys had been killed for any reason other than the obvious one: she must have seen something suspicious the previous morning. That meant another round of interviews with yesterday's suspects was a matter of urgency.

His interview with Julia and the others produced the unexpected news that their last sight of Gladys was of her getting
under the feet of Lady Clark and her son Nigel as they loaded
up Sir Nicholas's private possessions into a cardboard box.

'Ring Lady Clark,' he told Romford. 'Explain what has happened, postpone my meeting with her until tomorrow and get
from her a precise statement of her movements at lunch-time
today. And talk to the son as well.'

He called Amiss in and had a formal conversation with him
which established his alibi beyond doubt. 'I should be grateful,
sir,' he said, 'if you would find out when I can have a word with
the Secretary of State, the Parliamentary Under-Secretary of
State and Mr Parkinson.'

Amiss scurried off, glad to have something to take his
mind off his unreasonable guilt. Within a few minutes he had
produced Richard Parkinson, who could offer no alibi for the
critical period other than a phone call, which he had taken in
his office at 1.20. 'I'm sorry, Superintendent,' he said ruefully,
'but today I seized the chance to have a sandwich in the office
with the newspapers rather than go out. It seems to have been
another of my bad decisions.'

Milton dismissed him with a few comforting words and
found to his surprise that William Wells was now being ushered
into his office. He felt a grim satisfaction that Wells was worried
enough to make the concession of leaving his home territory for
the convenience of the police. He was looking a lot less confident than he had earlier, and he seemed to diminish in size as
he admitted that he had been alone in his office until he left at
1.15 for a late lunch. Could anyone testify that he had left at
1.15? Possibly his Private Secretary and one of the doormen.

Milton let him go and Amiss came in to explain that the
Secretary of State was in his office at the House of Commons and
would be at Milton's disposal at any time during the next hour.

Milton debated sending a sergeant over to see Nixon and
thought better of it. He wanted to get to know all his suspects
as well as possible, and he might be able to spot a change

of expression, some nuance that another might miss. He left Romford and Pike with a long list of instructions and walked quickly over to the Commons. At rush-hour it was foolish to take a car.

He bypassed the queues of tourists waiting to get into the House and identified himself to one of the policemen inside. Conducted swiftly and deferentially towards Nixon's quarters, Milton had time to cast a quick look over the marble, the statues, the carved ceiling and the acres of space which made the lobby of the House magically redolent of history and power. He could understand how a place like this could exercise such a hold over its occupants. It wouldn't be hard to feel part of a noble tradition, and it wouldn't be long before you began to feel yourself a worthy descendant of the famous whose busts lay scattered about in the alcoves. How could you work in such an environment, with all its arcane customs conspiring to make you feel part of an élite, without eventually believing that that truly made you special? How did M.P.s, let alone ministers, keep any sense of what preoccupied the man-in-the-street? Milton didn't know. He supposed they didn't and never had. Why should they? Parliament had got on well enough without ever worrying about much that went on outside its own walls—except at election time. Maybe if you truly kept in touch with reality the sheer artificiality of the House would drive you mad.

He arrived at Nixon's door and was ushered in by his escort. Even he, Milton noticed, seemed to have taken on the colour of the place. He was more like a butler than a policeman. Nixon greeted him warmly—almost like a friend—and Milton felt unnerved by the thought that he was here to upset him again. A man could hardly be expected to relish the experience of having his Father Confessor suddenly turn up accusing him by implication of fresh sins. He decided to go straight to the point.

'I'm sorry to trouble you, sir, but we've had another murder.'

'I know, Superintendent,' said Nixon quietly. 'An unfortunate woman has been found knifed. You are obviously bound to assume that there is a connection with yesterday's events, and you want to know if I have an alibi.'

'Exactly, sir,' said Milton, thankful that Nixon hadn't lapsed into politicianese. 'Can you tell me what you were doing at lunchtime today?'

He saw a look of alarm cross Nixon's face. 'Until one o'clock I was in my office with Douglas Sanders, Sir Nicholas's successor. From then onwards, I stayed alone for an hour, having given strict instructions that I wasn't to be disturbed. You see, Superintendent, since yesterday I haven't had any time at all to myself for private reflection. I had to decide what, if anything, I was going to do to try to retrieve my reputation after the events of yesterday morning. Specifically, I was considering whether it would be wise to confide to the Chancellor the role Sir Nicholas had played or whether I should simply brazen it out.'

'It's not strictly germane, sir, but could I ask what you decided?'

'To let the whole thing drop. News of my incompetence will get back to the Prime Minister and will make it easier for me to resign at the next reshuffle. In the unlikely event of my being able to clear myself of the charge of bungling an important meeting, the Prime Minister would probably want to keep me on, and I would find it very hard to resist any appeal he might make to my loyalty. You may find it hard to believe, Superintendent, in view of what I told you yesterday about my handling of my job, but he does value me as a Cabinet colleague. You see, I am one of the very few who have no further personal ambition. He can, therefore, rely on me to give him unqualified support on most issues. Many of my colleagues have a permanent eye on the main chance. It often leads them to take up unrealistic positions in Cabinet, leak accounts of arguments which show them in a good electoral light, and bargain for departmental gain with covert threats of resignation. However, the Prime Minister, with an election not far away, cannot afford to have anyone in the Cabinet who does not have the respect of influential people—so although I am clear on these other counts, the impossibility of my rapidly regaining the esteem of the Establishment means the P.M. will be delighted if I resign—which I shall do for trumped-up personal reasons.'

'That, if I may say so, sir, is a courageous decision.'

'Not really, Superintendent. You see, while you're a minister you can't bear the thought of being out of office. However severe the demands made on you, almost every hour of the day you get some fillips to your ego. You are surrounded by comfort and deference. You never have to make decisions about what you will do, where you will go or how to organize the practical side of life. Certainly, you are supposed to make major decisions. But if you have no ambitions to master your department, your civil servants will politely steer you towards the decision they favour. I suppose it's like being a member of the Royal Family. There is room for individual initiative, but if you are content to go along with the system, it carries you along with it. You adopt your civil servants' policies, speak their lines, perform when you're told to perform and turn into a well-looked-after puppet. It's only when you get a shock of the kind I experienced yesterday that you begin to question whether it's a worthwhile occupation. I have decided that, for me, it isn't.'

Milton pulled himself together. He was getting too much involved in this. He was here to check Nixon's movements, not to take part in a discussion on his moment of truth. After all, he could be responsible for that pathetic corpse behind the sofa. 'Thank you for telling me, sir, but I'm afraid I must go back to lunchtime today.'

'Of course, Superintendent. I apologise for this flood of confidences. It's just that it has been such a relief to talk frankly to someone for a change. What do you need to know?'

'Did anyone see you during the hour you were alone in your office?'

'No. And let me anticipate your next question. I could have left the room without being observed, since I have a door which leads out into the corridor. May I ask when the murder took place?'

'Between one and one thirty, sir.'

'And in the Permanent Secretary's office next door to my room over there, I hear?'

'Yes, sir,' said Milton unhappily.

'Well, Superintendent, I can't pretend that this isn't frightening. I can only hope that at least one of your suspects—the one who killed her—is in the same position as myself.'

'Some are, sir,' said Milton unprofessionally, 'but I should be grateful if you would keep that to yourself until you hear it from another source.'

As they shook hands warmly, Milton tried unsuccessfully to repress his hope that Nixon was simply what he seemed—an honest man caught in a web of circumstances beyond his control.

He headed back to the department.

Tuesday Evening

Chapter Fifteen

It was almost 9.00 when Milton joined Amiss in the corner of the curry house. He had had a great deal of trouble in fobbing off the reporters surrounding the departmental building, but harassed as he was, he saw with concern that his companion was still looking very shaken. He had been reading an evening paper—a late edition which screamed the headline 'MANIAC IN WHITEHALL?', and he had obviously begun to drown his sorrows.

'Are you sure you're up to this conversation, Robert?' he asked anxiously. 'Wouldn't you be better off going home and getting some sleep?'

'Look, Jim, I live alone in a small flat near the office. It's awash with dirty socks and stale half-loaves of bread. If I go home to it now in my present state of mind I'll drink myself into oblivion and be no use to you tomorrow.'

'If you're sure. Don't you have any friends you can go to?'

'I don't have much time for friends any more. You don't have much of a social life if you rarely leave the office before half eight and frequently have to be away at weekends. People get tired of your unreliability. They put it down to self-importance. Besides, most of my university friends think I have sold out and have dropped me for reasons of the highest principle. Most of my socializing is with other Private Secretaries, and we don't even know if we like each other. We just enjoy each others' company because we have a lot in common and can be irreverent and indiscreet without fearing the consequences.'

'No girlfriends?'

'After the last one decamped because she couldn't stand the way my work dominated my life, I've decided to avoid involvements until I move to a less demanding job. I'll be monkish for a few months yet.'

Milton sympathized. After all, how many friends did he have outside the force—or even in it? He had become inured over the years to the distaste people felt for socializing with the police. He wasn't really surprised to hear that Amiss's generation reacted much the same way to civil servants.

He ordered a large drink and a meal. He was relieved to see that alcohol didn't seem to affect Amiss's articulacy and he managed to persuade him to eat something. Rice was terrific for soaking up gin.

'Well, first of all, thanks for getting that message to me. It's immensely useful.'

'Your wife is very pleasant.'

'She is,' said Milton, suppressing an ache to spend an evening with her alone. The quicker he got this case over and done with the better. 'Tell me how you got hold of the information about Jenkins and Lady Clark.'

Amiss told him about his researches of the morning.

'I'm very grateful. I didn't expect you to go to so much trouble.'

'I'm ashamed to say I enjoyed it, Jim. I'm getting a taste for idle gossip like most of them. Maybe it's just a way of compensating for the extreme discretion we are supposed to show in our work. We have to keep so much of what we do secret that we tend to let ourselves go in speculation about what our colleagues get up to privately. It's a relief to be able to turn that gossip to practical effect for once.'

'Well, in that case, keep digging. Though I don't suppose there's much else you can find out. Now it's my turn.'

Milton gave an account of his main interviews of the day. He felt a qualm about breaking Nixon's confidence, but he was sure enough of Amiss by now to know that he was too compassionate to leak something as intensely personal as this into the Private Secretary network. Amiss's reaction was as he expected.

'The poor bugger. It's been worse even than I imagined. I'm not surprised that so many politicians hate civil servants. It only takes one destructive one to ruin the reputation of the rest of us.'

'It still amazes me that anyone could get away with what Sir Nicholas got away with.'

'Well, of course, that was a special case. Sir Nicholas was unusually nasty as well as very clever and Nixon was extremely vulnerable. But other politicians have occasional bad experiences as well. You see, as you've realized by now, you don't have to be clever to be a minister, but you can't rise to be a top civil servant without being very clever indeed. You can be negative, unimaginative and a bad manager but you've got to be able to reduce immense masses of material to comprehensible, lucid prose; you've got to be able to become an instant expert on the most obscure problems overnight; you've got to be able to churn out complex briefing at short notice; and you've got to be able to spot in the most bland and innocuous statements long-range policy implications for your department.'

'It all sounds a bit like making a life's work of those comprehension passages you get in school exams.'

'You've got it perfectly, Jim. A great part of our work is *précis* writing at a superior level. The ability to justify the same policy in one sentence, a three-hundred-word press statement, a two-thousand-word brief or a five-thousand-word speech is a prerequisite of success. It's very easy to impress outsiders with the command the civil service has of the written and spoken word. Few politicians can compete on paper; some are fine speakers, but rhetoric is of no use in small committees. You don't find many Presidents of the Oxford Union going into the civil service. We attract the kind of people who were at their best defending their essays to their tutors.'

'How can politicians possibly master their departments, then?'

'Most of them can't. Perhaps a couple in every administration. And they are invariably people who can beat the civil servants at their own game by absorbing information at lightning speed and using it for their own ends. It also helps to be a bully. We don't like being shouted at.'

'More and more, I feel for Nixon,' said Milton.

'Yes, me too. I hope we don't find we drove him to murder in the end.'

'Well, he's in a worse position now than yesterday, I'm afraid. Since I left him I've been looking at all the evidence we've got on the whereabouts of the obvious suspects. Our short list is down to Nixon, Wells and Parkinson, with Shaw and Stafford possibles. Either of those two would have had to get hold of a pass into the building from somewhere, though, and it seems hard to imagine how they could have found their way to your office and Gladys without being spotted. How could they even have recognized Gladys yesterday?—unless they were introduced to her by Sir Nicholas.'

'No chance of that. Sir Nicholas didn't go in for that sort of courtesy with Clerical Assistants.'

'Anyway, given what you've told me about Shaw's relationship with Sir Nicholas, there doesn't seem to be a motive worth considering in his case.'

'Unless it's class warfare.'

Milton treated that remark with the contempt it deserved.

'So the other two on your shortlist have alibis?' asked Amiss.

'Right. Unshakable ones from what I've heard.'

'What about Lady Clark and her son? Did they have anything useful to say?'

'Only that they left the office at about five past one. That's confirmed by the visitors' passes they handed in on their way out, which show that they left the building at ten past one.'

'There's no chance, I suppose, that they killed Gladys in order to protect Jenkins?'

'Nigel Clark would have had to have an Oedipus complex of spectacular proportions to connive at the killing of Gladys to protect his father's murderer.'

'Well, you never know,' said Amiss hopefully. 'Maybe he inherited his father's mean streak. And God knows what kind of a parent Sir Nicholas was. I must see what I can find out about that.'

'I'd be interested in anything you pick up about him. I'll be seeing him tomorrow morning when I visit his mother. It'll be a change, anyway, to see a female suspect. There are too many men in this case. Where are all the senior female civil servants? I've been meaning to ask you.'

'We've only a tiny number in this department. Senior women tend to be pushed towards departments dealing with education or the social services. The same thing happens with female politicians. It's an expression of the old conviction that they can't cope with anything vaguely technical like energy, industry or whatever. It's amazing really when you consider that a history graduate like me—who can't change a bicycle tyre—can be put without a thought into a job dealing with plastics recycling. It's even more remarkable when you know that, apart from appearance, senior female officials are indistinguishable from their male counterparts. We've got a lot of old women in the service, but the majority of them are men. We've also got a smaller number of thrusting dynamic people with balls, but there are women among their number too. I suppose one reason for discriminating against them is that there's a general view that industrialists or trades unionists will have a seizure if they're confronted by a woman in a position of responsibility. Miss Beckett's our token woman. Maybe she'll blaze a trail by proving that she's a good chap.'

'You seem very bitter about the civil service, Robert. Why do you stay in it?'

'I'm literate and articulate, and I can do well there if I can also learn to be a bureaucrat. That's the difficult bit. When I move to a more mundane job I'll have all the crap of inter-departmental jealousies and niggling memoranda flying round like confetti. I don't know if I'll be able to stick it then. The trouble is, there isn't any other job I can think of that doesn't have even more unattractive aspects, and fewer intelligent people to play silly games with.'

Milton didn't have any helpful suggestions to offer. Amiss seemed to be in a bleak mood. Perhaps he shouldn't be taken too seriously tonight.

Amiss fell silent and ordered another drink. He caught Milton's concerned look and gave a forced smile.

'Don't worry. I'm not going to crack up. It's just that my generation isn't used to death. Sanders was in the war and probably saw far worse sights than poor old Gladys. We've been protected from all of that. How did you come to terms with it, Jim? You can't have seen many before you joined the police.'

Milton explained what the sight of his first corpse had done to him. He had been sick for hours after having been called out to a particularly gruesome car crash. 'But you get used to it in no time. You find yourself making sick jokes to protect yourself from the horror of what you are seeing.'

'It's interesting, isn't it, that last night you were the one who was being shocked? You seemed to be horrified by all the things I take for granted—the fact that civil servants can be venal and politicians stupid.'

'That makes me seem more naïve than I think I am. It was just that I'd never thought about it before. I've never been politically partisan. I don't believe that either side has the monopoly of right. Very committed people worry me, whether they're represented by the occasional National Front copper or a paranoid Trotskyite demonstrator. I prefer to get on with my job. I suppose I've been shocked by the discovery that politicians have so little power and that we expect them to be super-human, while insisting they be representative of their electorate.'

'At least we can be grateful to the murderer for giving us both the opportunity to broaden our minds,' said Amiss, calling for the bill. 'Same place, same sort of time tomorrow?'

'I look forward to it,' said Milton, finding to his surprise that it was the truth.

Wednesday Morning

Chapter Sixteen

'Come on, darling. Give me a professional view. Is it conceivable that Nigel Clark might have agreed to protect his mother's lover by involving himself in murder?'

'It's not the kind of problem I come up against much in a management consultancy,' said Ann Milton, wrinkling her forehead. 'It's a long time since I studied the psychology of the family. My guess would be that it's almost impossible. Sons who love their mothers that much are unlikely to encourage them to have lovers. Now, if it were the other way round it would be different. There's no love more ruthless than that of a mother.'

'I thought you'd say that,' said her husband, 'but the security on Monday in Embankment Tower was so ferocious that Nigel couldn't have got in without having been vouched for by someone working there. That would have been on record, and it isn't.'

'Well, I wish you luck,' said Ann, draining the last of her coffee and jumping to her feet. 'I hope Deep Throat doesn't want to get in touch with me this morning. I've got a meeting in half an hour and it's likely to go on all morning.'

'I shouldn't think there's any danger of that. I can't really expect him to deliver any more nuggets. He's already saved me days of work.'

'Any chance of finding your murderer this week? We could take a few days off and go to Paris for a long weekend.'

'The last time we planned that you had to cancel because someone at work got sick.'

'True. And the time before you had to cancel because of a panic about IRA bombs.'

They both sighed. 'Damn it,' said Milton. 'We'll never get there if we don't keep trying. It'll give me an added incentive. Not that I really need one. Book tickets provisionally for Saturday morning and I'll let you know on Thursday evening if we can go ahead.'

Ann went off with a spring in her step, which Milton gloomily recorded as another triumph of hope over experience. The chances of disentangling this one quickly had to be slim indeed. He wondered bitterly how a floor so stuffed with people could yield no one who had been in the corridor at the moment when the murderer slipped in or out of Gladys's office.

Even St James's Park couldn't help that morning, though Milton spent a couple of minutes staring conscientiously at the splashings of the ducks in an effort to lighten his mood. His morning conference with his superiors didn't help much. Although the Assistant Commissioner was clearly impressed by the way in which Milton had managed to get so much out of the suspects he had interviewed, he was in one of those panics to which he was subject when a case was grabbing the headlines. The popular papers were enjoying themselves hugely, and were all carrying interviews with Gladys's husband. The A.C. didn't like the tone of them. 'Seems like a surly brute.'

'Well, sir. You can hardly expect him to be very happy about his wife's death.'

'Of course not. But I don't like his remarks about his wife having been murdered by some nob.'

'I'm afraid he's probably right,' said Milton. 'It's a pretty distinguished short-list.'

'The Commissioner's been on again,' said the A.C. 'The Prime Minister is demanding a quick conclusion to the whole business and wants to know if we've got our best men on the job. I must tell you plainly that I thought again about putting a Chief Superintendent onto it, but I've decided against it. Nobody could have got more out of those people yesterday than you did. I'm very surprised. I'd have expected them to try to cover things up more. You must have played the interrogations very well.'

Milton tried to look modest. 'I expect I was just lucky in what I asked them, sir,' he said, hoping he wouldn't be believed, and that it would indeed be put down to god-like intuition.

'Nothing else we can usefully talk about then?' asked the A.C. 'Who are you seeing next?'

'Gladys Bradley's husband; Lady Clark and her son; and Alfred Shaw and Martin Jenkins. I don't need to see Stafford at the moment. I had a very open discussion with him yesterday.'

'Why are you bothering about Jenkins? He couldn't have killed Mrs Bradley.'

'There's just that possible link-up with Lady Clark,' said Milton apologetically.

'Oh, that. You're surely not going to believe a silly piece of malice like that postcard. Someone's trying to draw you off the proper scent, or, more likely, it's somebody's idea of a joke and nothing whatever to do with the case.'

'I'm sure you're right, sir, but I wouldn't feel easy unless I checked up on it.'

'If you must. But go easily now. I don't want either of them upset. You haven't forgotten the way Jenkins carried on over the fights between the police and a few of his members on the picket-line in Colchester last year.'

'No, sir,' said Milton, gritting his teeth. 'I haven't forgotten.'

'All right. Carry on. But for God's sake don't let there be any more murders.'

The A.C. must be in a real state of jitters if he's coming out with that sort of stuff, Milton reflected charitably as he began to shuffle papers back at his own desk. How the hell was he supposed to get any information out of Lady Clark or Jenkins if he was worrying about possible complaints? And sweet Jesus, how was he to stop any more murders without locking up all the suspects? It would be highly popular with the Prime Minister if he locked up Nixon, Wells, Parkinson and, to be on the safe side, Alf Shaw, Stafford, Jenkins, Lady Clark and Nigel. He sloughed off his self-pity. If Amiss could take risks with his career, so could he.

Chapter Seventeen

Mr Bradley was, if anything, worse than Milton had expected from the accounts he had heard. He was a large, angry-looking man, with rather spiteful little eyes. Milton had become so accustomed in only a couple of days to the suavity of the people he had had to interview that he was momentarily taken aback by Bradley's belligerence. He was subjected to a tirade on his incompetence in letting murderers run loose around the place looking for innocent victims before he was finally, grudgingly led into the front room of the little terraced house.

It was incredibly untidy. Women's magazines, paperback romances, empty beer bottles, knitting patterns, piles of laundry and old copies of racing papers jostled each other on all available surfaces. Gladys was obviously no more efficient here than at work, he thought, though from the indifference Bradley exhibited in shoving a pile of odds and ends off an armchair, it didn't seem as if she had much incentive to be house-proud. He felt that sense of depression which always gripped him at the sight of the personal belongings of someone who has died unexpectedly. The muddy-coloured piece of knitting at his feet was bad enough; the chastely-kissing couples on the covers of the romantic novels were worse. And the complete charmlessness of Bradley made Gladys's life seem too pathetic to be contemplated.

He thought Bradley was going to hit him when he asked where he had been at lunchtime the previous day.

'My old woman is killed by some fucking lunatic up there and you have the nerve to ask me what I was doing. I suppose you think I killed that Clark as well. Maybe you think I thought they were having it off. I don't have to put up with this fucking treatment. Get out of here.'

It took all Milton's much-vaunted tact to quieten him down and convince him that these were merely routine questions. Bradley eventually admitted to having spent lunchtime in the neighbouring pub with a couple of mates. He didn't have a job at the moment. Had to rely on the wife's pay packet. Wouldn't even have that now, he added.

And you couldn't even bother to tidy up the house or do the shopping while she was at work, Milton wanted to say. The fellow was a monster. Oafish, brutal, greedy and lazy. Instead he took the names of the men Bradley had been with and began to ask him if Gladys had said anything about her meeting with Sir Nicholas on Monday morning.

Bradley threw up his hands. 'How can I be expected to remember everything she rabbited on about. Half the time none of it made sense.'

'If you could just cast your mind back to Monday night, sir, I would be greatly obliged. We are reasonably sure that whoever killed your wife also killed Sir Nicholas, and she must have seen or heard something that made her a threat to the murderer.'

Bradley sat and thought for a minute or two. In repose his face was different—almost pleasant. He might be quite amiable in the pub, thought Milton.

'She said something about a row.'

'With whom, sir?'

'No. She didn't have the row. She heard some fellow arguing with Clark about something. I don't remember what it was about. I was watching television at the time and she was just going on.'

'Can you remember anything at all, sir?'

'She said something like that she was so embarrassed because she didn't know whether to go into the room or not. She was supposed to see him and she could hear him from the corridor.'

'Did she see who it was with Clark?'

'Don't remember.'

Milton pressed on for a while, but he eventually realized that Bradley wasn't going to come up with any more. If Gladys had mentioned any names, Bradley hadn't listened. There was no point in going on. He promised to let Milton know if he remembered anything else, but made it clear that there wasn't a cat in hell's chance of his doing so.

Milton got up to go. Bradley looked up and said unexpectedly. 'She looked all right when I had to identify her last night. As if she didn't know what happened. Do you think she knew what was going to be done to her?'

'No, sir. I'm sure she didn't.'

'Nobody told me how it happened.'

'We're pretty clear that she walked into the room with the murderer of her own free will and that she was stabbed from behind as she was looking out of the window.'

'You mean this geezer was someone she knew?'

'Well, if not knew, would have trusted because he seemed all right.'

'You're telling me that she trusted someone she had heard arguing with Clark a few minutes before he was murdered?'

'Perhaps she didn't realize the implications, sir.'

'The poor stupid bitch,' said Bradley. 'The poor stupid bitch. She didn't know anything, did she? She went on about how nice it was to work with gentlemen. Nearest thing she ever got to one of her bloody silly love books.' And to Milton's consternation, he began to cry.

It was many long minutes before he wiped his eyes and pulled himself together. Milton thought he must never have cried before—he was so incapable of controlling it. He kept repeating 'poor stupid bitch' through his tears and Milton realized it was an endearment. When he finally looked up he asked simply, 'What am I going to do on my own?'

Milton couldn't cope. He could only hope that some of his mates would rise to the occasion and restore Bradley to his old aggressive self. He could offer nothing except platitudes which made him wince. He walked away from the mean little house with a feeling of release and wonder at the many forms in which love manifested itself. At least Amiss would be glad to know that there was somebody who would miss Gladys.

Chapter Eighteen

Lady Clark's welcome was as different from Bradley's as was her house. She greeted him in a reserved but courteous way on the threshold of her elegant Georgian house in a South Kensington square.

Sir Nicholas certainly had taste. Milton gave him that. Classy was the word. A classy wife and a classy house. She was a bit insipid for his taste, the blonde hair and the eyes a bit too light, the features a bit too narrow and the manner a bit too apologetic. But she certainly had style.

So had the interior of the house. Milton had seen it a hundred times in glossy magazines. Pale walls, good furniture, curtains and sofa coverings blended subtly and seemed to enhance each other. There were stretches of highly polished surfaces bearing innumerable pieces of expensive-looking silver and pottery. Not a reproduction in sight, thought Milton, looking round at the watercolours which dominated two of the walls. There had to be money here as well as taste. Surely you couldn't produce that sort of effect on even a senior civil-servant's salary. He knew they were always being accused of bleeding the country white, but they couldn't be doing it to the level necessary to finance this. This house stank of money—it had to be inherited. Was it the wife's? He didn't think Sir Nicholas came from that sort of background. In a cursory glance at *Who's Who* he had noticed that he had been educated at a state school—a fact which had surprised him at the time since he had a vague belief that all top civil servants were public-school chaps.

Lady Clark put him sitting in one of the mustard sofas and offered him coffee. Milton accepted gratefully. He was still feeling some emotional exhaustion from his interview with Bradley. She disappeared. He wondered if the establishment ran to servants, and decided not. With the shortage of domestics these days it would be hard to imagine one staying in a house which contained Sir Nicholas. A daily cleaning woman, maybe, who could be kept away from him.

Lady Clark re-entered carrying a silver tray. The cups, Milton noted apprehensively, were small and looked valuable. His and Ann's taste lay more towards objects that you didn't mind dropping. He hated the feeling of strain one got from handling other people's treasured possessions. He was inclined to be rather clumsy at the best of times, and the fear of breaking one of the cups or spilling coffee on the off-white wool carpet was going to take away any benefit he might have had from a quick injection of caffeine. His normal sense of proportion reasserted itself while she was plying him with biscuits. It was pretty silly to worry about spoiling someone's carpet when you should be worrying instead about how to ask them about a love affair you weren't supposed to know about.

He asked her first if she had any idea of who might have wanted to kill her husband. She didn't. Nicholas could, she admitted, sometimes be a bit difficult. She had a feeling that he didn't get on with all his colleagues. But then, who did?

Cul-de-sac number one, thought Milton. Then he had his flash of inspiration.

'Did he often bring work home from the office?'

'Oh, yes. All the time. He worked very hard.'

'Can you tell me if he brought any work home last weekend?'

'Yes, he did. He had to write a speech for his Secretary of State. I don't really understand why. I thought he had lots of staff to do that kind of thing.'

'Could he type, Lady Clark?'

'Oh, no. But I used to type things for him sometimes. I was a secretary once. I typed out the speech for him on Sunday.'

'I'm sorry to ask you this, but could I see any notes he left? I'm anxious to get all possible details on what he was doing during the days immediately preceding his death.'

Lady Clark was too well-trained to question this. She led him obediently to Sir Nicholas's study. He looked round, hoping for some kind of insight into the man whose behaviour was still puzzling him. What were his most private and treasured possessions? What kind of books did he read? Was he as ascetic in private life as he seemed to be in public?

First he had to go throught the motions of looking through the notes for the speech. He wasn't surprised by what he found. The original—correct—speech was lying neatly on the desk beside an immaculately handwritten sheaf of papers. He looked quickly through the two versions and saw the differences in figures, the changes of emphasis and all the other alterations that Amiss had told him about.

'I don't see the typewriter.'

'Oh, no. That's in my room. Nicholas couldn't bear the noise and in any case he liked to be entirely private in here. It's one of those golfball machines, you know. The ones with the replaceable typefaces. We had to have one of those because Nicholas used Greek quite a lot. I'm afraid I was a bit stupid with the Greek. I always thought it would be easier for everyone if he used English all the time.'

'Do you mind if I look around? You never know where you may find a clue,' he said fatuously. Lady Clark was impressed. 'I'll leave you here for a while, Superintendent. Come and join me when you've finished.'

He looked appraisingly around the room. It was so different from the drawing-room that he was taken aback. Perhaps that reflected her personality and this his. If so, he was a strange man indeed. There was a whole wall of paintings—mostly reproductions here—which Milton found profoundly disturbing. Munch he recognized. And a Grosz. He disliked both of them. But if their view of the world seemed a bit bleak, they were positively cheery beside some of the ones he didn't recognize. He looked closely at a violently depicted mouth out of which seemed to be coming screams of agony. Francis Bacon. Agony and despair. Of course. That was the keynote of the collection. Was he simply a sadist? No. Amiss had said something about Sir Nicholas's pastime being pulling wings off Assistant Secretaries, but that seemed to be more a matter of expressing disdain for his intellectual inferiors. Certainly there were no dismembered limbs in his picture collection—no Bosch, no Goya.

He gave up on the pictures and turned to the bookcases. A long row of reference books. That was to be expected. So was what looked to be a fine collection of Greek and Latin authors. Shelves full of biographies—mainly political. A surprisingly large collection of works on philosophy and religion. He looked in vain for English literature. There didn't seem to be a novel or a poem anywhere. Not rigorous enough intellectually, he supposed.

He looked idly through a shelf of records and found them as perplexingly unfamiliar as many of the pictures. The collection seemed to be comprised (with the exception of a great deal of Bach) of modern composers, to whose music Milton never listened if he could possibly avoid it. But he could hardly be surprised that Sir Nicholas preferred dissonance to harmony.

There was only the desk to be looked at now. The rest of the study was sparse. Angular sculptures were dotted about here and there. They bore a close resemblance to the one which had finally done for Sir Nicholas. Milton looked quickly through the drawers of the desk. He could find nothing personal—only various kinds of stationery. He took one final look around, shuddered again at the pictures and rejoined Lady Clark.

'Did you find anything, Superintendent?' she asked brightly.

'I don't think so, Lady Clark. I must say I prefer the pictures you've got here to those in Sir Nicholas's room.'

'Oh, we didn't have the same taste at all in things like that. I suppose I'm not intelligent enought to understand the sort of thing Nicholas liked.'

Milton was sitting silently.

'Is there anything else I can help you with, Superintendent?'

'Several things, Lady Clark. To begin with, did you notice anything different about Sir Nicholas's mood during the weekend?'

'Just that he was in very good spirits. He was really pleased with the speech he wrote. He said he expected it to be very successful. It seemed rather dull to me, but I don't know anything about politics.'

'Let me tell you about that speech,' said Milton, and proceeded to give her the bare essentials of the story of the substitution.

She looked frightened. 'Surely it was a mistake. He wouldn't have done something as cruel as that to such a nice man as Harvey.'

'I'm afraid there's no doubt about it, ma'am.'

'You're not saying that Harvey …?'

'No, I'm not. He was not the only one present at that meeting who had been badly treated by your husband.'

He wondered if she would try being insulted—refusing to hear anything against the martyred husband. But she didn't. 'Archibald,' she said. 'I thought Nicholas was very hard to say to him what he did.'

'Mr Stafford?'

'Yes. You will know that he was going to lose his job. I heard Nicholas say to him on the phone that he should be man enough to know when he was past it.'

'Was such cruelty unusual in Sir Nicholas?'

'I don't know if we're using the right word, Superintendent. He had very high standards of behaviour, and he was hard on people who didn't live up to them. That meant he sometimes seemed cruel. But I don't think he realized what he was doing. It was disappointment really, I think.'

Milton thought of the Assistant Commissioner's warning and decided to disregard it.

'And did you live up to his high standards, Lady Clark?'

'I haven't for a long time,' she said, and to Milton's horror, like Bradley, she burst into tears.

Chapter Nineteen

As the sobs subsided, Milton prayed she wouldn't be clear-headed enough to realize that, as things stood, he had no right to ask her to tell him about her marriage. She couldn't be suspected of having murdered Sir Nicholas, and she couldn't know that he was looking for a motive for Jenkins.

He needn't have worried. She held forth the way that Harvey Nixon had. Sir Nicholas had obviously succeeded in making his victims so tense that the first taste of the relief of being able to talk about what they had endured made them eager to get it all out.

'We met nearly thirty years ago in Oxford. My brother was an undergraduate acquaintance of Nicholas's, and he introduced us at a party he gave one weekend in January.'

'Were you an undergraduate too?'

'Oh, no. I was never much good academically. I had just started work in London as a secretary. I was only seventeen. Nicholas was almost twenty-three. He'd done his time in the army and was now in his final year. He was very clever, very glamorous and very attractive.'

Milton's face must have betrayed his surprise at such a description of the desiccated face he had seen in death. She got up and pulled a photograph album from a cupboard.

'Would you like to see a picture of us on our wedding-day?'

Milton looked with astonishment at the two happy faces which smiled confidently at him. The pretty blond girl sparkled at the dark and powerful young man at her side. He wasn't hand-some, but the humorous set of his mouth and the laughter in his eyes gave him an almost raffish attraction. He handed the album back without speaking.

'You wouldn't have recognized him, would you, Superin-tendent? For many years I've had to rely on that photograph to remind me of what we used to be like.'

'You looked as if you were both very much in love.'

'Oh, we were. We couldn't see enough of each other. I used to go up to Oxford nearly every weekend and we had one of those magical summer terms of sun and parties and punting. Nicholas was so clever he didn't need to work terribly hard. He got the best First of his year in Greats.'

'When did you marry?'

'A month after he graduated. It was a silly thing to do. We'd never done anything together except enjoy ourselves. We'd never had to face any problems. Yet Nicholas didn't want to wait and I couldn't think of anything except what joy it would be to be together all the time.'

'Did he join the civil service immediately?'

'No. Not until the following year. We had decided to give him a couple of years to try to find a seat.'

'He wanted to go into politics?' asked Milton, incredulously.

'Oh, very much. Nicholas was very radical in those days. He wanted to reform the world. He was an active socialist all the time he was at Oxford. You see, his father's business had failed during the thirties and Nicholas had known what poverty was like. He used to shock my father with some of his ideas. Daddy was pretty well off and he didn't like Nicholas's talk about the cor-ruption of the capitalist system. They got on quite well, though. Nicholas was so charming he could get round anyone.'

Milton wondered wildly if they were talking about the same Nicholas.

'You're looking as though you don't believe me, Superintendent, and I don't blame you. I often haven't myself been able to believe the change in him.'

'What went wrong?'

'Money, really. We hadn't got much to live on. I had gone on working and Nicholas was teaching at a crammer. He was spending a lot of his spare time in Labour party work and the prospects of getting a seat seemed reasonably good. Then I got pregnant and had to give up work.'

'You couldn't live on his salary?'

'We probably could have managed. I wouldn't have minded. But Daddy got at Nicholas about getting a proper job and keeping his wife and child decently. Nicholas was very proud and couldn't bear to think I might regret the comforts of the old days. I couldn't convince him that all I cared about was being with him. He made up his mind—and when he did that you couldn't shift him. He applied for a number of jobs and the best one that came up was in the civil service. He had only been there a couple of weeks when I lost the baby.'

'Couldn't he have left the job then?'

'He wouldn't. He'd had to give up active politics when he joined and he wouldn't go back. He had a very obstinate streak. He insisted that he had made his decision and would stick to it. He threw himself instead into making a success of his job. He'd been very upset about the baby, and work seemed to be the only thing that took his mind off it.'

'What did you do?'

'I didn't go back to work. It wasn't really respectable for a middle-class married woman to work in those days and Daddy backed up Nicholas when he said there was no need for me to get a job now that he was earning a decent salary. Anyway, we assumed it wouldn't be long before I became pregnant again.

'During the next five years I miscarried twice and I was ill a lot. It was hard on Nicholas. He worked very long hours and I was a worry rather than a pleasure to him. That was when the disappointment began to show.'

'But it wasn't your fault.'

'No. But Nicholas had already made one big sacrifice. His life was being disrupted by my endless illnesses. He desperately

wanted children, and I couldn't give them to him. It would have
taken a very understanding man to feel no resentment of me.'

'Didn't it make a difference when Nigel was born?'

'Oh, yes. For a while. But I had such a hard time with the
birth that I was warned I shouldn't have any more, and that was
another disappointment. And although Nicholas was mad about
Nigel, he wasn't really much good with him. He was always trying
to teach him and make him read when he just wanted to play.
Nicholas knew that Nigel was much more fond of me.'

'Wasn't his success at work any compensation?'

'It helped, but work brought its own problems. Of course,
Nicholas was so clever that he got on very quickly, but he always
seemed to crave more recognition than he got. Although he
didn't talk about it much, I noticed him being very bitter when
others his own age were promoted earlier.'

'He got to the top eventually, though.'

'It depends what you call the top. Nicholas really wanted to head
a bigger department. The Department of Conservation isn't very
important. It was hived off from the Department of Energy.'

'What about your lives together?'

'He grew more and more distant. When I inherited money
and we could afford to buy this house and furnish it as we liked.
I thought it would make a difference. It is very central and I
had visions of being able to entertain a lot. Nicholas didn't take
much interest in the house, though. He left it to me to do what I
wanted to it. He spent more and more time in his study, reading
and working. He didn't want to entertain—just to be left alone.
We just had the odd few dinners when he thought it would be
useful to talk informally to colleagues or politicians.'

'What about friends?'

'We didn't have many. Nicholas kept up with a few of his
independently. He seemed to prefer to have lunch with them
rather than bring them home. I thought he was rather ashamed
of me. He despised the kind of thing I read and was always telling
me that my political views were ill-informed and naïve. I had
never been as left-wing as he was in the early days, but I stayed

loyal to the Labour party. He used to say that they were all fools and that he had been a fool as well ever to have thought that politics was an occupation for anyone with a brain.'

'What about Nigel?'

'I'm afraid he let Nicholas down by taking after me academically. God knows what his education cost. The school fees were enormous and he used to have private tuition in the holidays, but it didn't make any difference. By most people's standards he was bright enough. He went to university and got a second in Physics. But he was always a bit of a disappointment to Nicholas. He was hopeless at Classics and he was turned down by Oxford.'

'They got on badly, then?'

'Oh, no. They just didn't have much to do with one another.'

'Does Nigel live with you?'

'He did for a while after university, but he's just moved out. He's come back to stay with me for a while now.'

'I need to see him. Is he at work?'

'No. He's just gone over to collect a few things from his flat. He should be back any minute.'

Milton braced himself.

'I'm sorry to have to ask you such a personal question, Lady Clark, but is it true that you are involved with Martin Jenkins?'

Chapter Twenty

'Is this what you've been leading up to all this time?' she asked bitterly.

'Look, Lady Clark. I know this is unpleasant for you, but it's just as unpleasant for me. I have to find out who murdered your husband and Mrs Bradley, and if I have to trample over people's private lives to do so, I will. You must understand that I can't ignore a link between you and someone who was at the Monday morning meeting with Sir Nicholas.'

She was hesitating.

'Just tell me the truth, Lady Clark. It'll save us all a lot of harassment in the long run.'

'You're right, Superintendent. You've been kind to me, and I appreciate it. I realize you wouldn't ask about Martin and me if you didn't have to. I'll tell you about it.'

'Thank you.'

'We met about ten months ago at a local Labour party meeting where Martin was giving a speech. I hadn't expected to like him. All I knew about him was that he was a trade-union leader with a line in fiery Welsh rhetoric. I went along to hear him with a friend of mine from the party because I had nothing better to do that evening. I enjoyed his speech, though it was a bit radical for me. Martin goes on a lot about Establishment conspiracies, you know.'

'I know.'

'But afterwards, when a group of us had adjourned for a drink, he was quite different. He made me laugh a lot, and that's something I haven't done much of for a long time. And he seemed to find me amusing too. We went on talking after the others had left and he treated me as if I were intelligent and well-informed. We even found we shared a secret liking for murder stories.'

She looked ruefully at Milton.

'When he suggested lunch, I couldn't bear to refuse. He had made me feel young and attractive again. I didn't tell Nicholas. I knew what he thought of Martin and I wouldn't have been able to bear the snide remarks. We met several times for lunch, and then for dinner and for the last six months we've been having an affair. We've kept it as quiet as possible, but it looks as if we haven't been very successful.'

'Did Sir Nicholas know?'

'I don't see how he could. He never took any interest in how I spent my time. I was going to tell him soon. I had promised Martin that when Nigel left home I would leave Nicholas and go and live with him.'

'Wouldn't that have caused a minor scandal?'

'I just didn't care any more, Superintendent. I've wasted an awful lot of my life on Nicholas, who didn't want me. Martin wants me desperately, and I want him.'

'I hope you'll be very happy.'

'Thank you, Superintendent. I think we will, although the decencies require me to play the bereaved widow for a few months. Nicholas's death has postponed our being together, you see. So you can't possibly think that Martin had any motive to kill him. Quite the reverse.'

They heard the front door opening and a young man came into the room. Lady Clark introduced her son. He was very like his mother—the same blond hair and narrow features. He didn't have her elegance, but by the standards of his generation he was spruce—a well-pressed check shirt and a sharp crease in his white cotton trousers.

'Did you want to see me, Superintendent?'

'Only for a moment, sir. I wanted to check your movements yesterday lunchtime.'

They both confirmed their statements of the previous day. Lady Clark anticipated Milton's request to be left alone with Nigel for a moment and found a reason to go to the kitchen.

'Have you any idea, sir, who might have had reason to kill your father?'

'No, Superintendent. Unless someone wanted his job. I can't imagine the usual motives applying in my father's case. He didn't indulge in torrid love affairs and he won't leave much money.'

'You'd be surprised what a wide range of motives lead people to kill, sir. What seems trivial to most of us can seem overwhelmingly important to some. You can't think of anything, however slight, that might have led to his death?'

'Honestly, no, Superintendent. I haven't had much to do with my father over the past few years. I've been away at university most of the time.'

'I understand you had just moved into your own flat. There wasn't a breach between you, was there?'

'Oh, no, Superintendent. I always wanted to live away from home and be independent as soon as I could afford to.'

'How were your relations with your father, sir?'

'Not very close, Superintendent. We weren't much alike. Didn't have a lot to talk about.'

'No rows?'

'Well, of course there were some disagreements, since our approach to life was so different. He hadn't got much time for my generation. Thought us frivolous and idle. But I went my way and he went his. Neither of us was the rowing type.'

'Very well, sir. Thank you. I don't think there's anything else I want to ask you.'

'I'll just call my mother.'

Lady Clark came in carrying another silver tray, on which rested this time three glasses and a decanter.

'Do have a glass of sherry with us before you leave, Superintendent?'

Milton accepted with some secret amusement. Amiss had confided in him the previous night, when ordering drinks, that he was looked on askance by some colleagues because he couldn't stand sherry (the traditional tipple at in-house get-togethers) and had provided gin instead for a Christmas office drink. Apparently the effect on Gladys had been dramatic. She had shown an unexpected talent for singing old Rosemary Clooney numbers. Milton didn't care for sherry much either, but he knew a symbolic drink when he saw one. Lady Clark was showing her appreciation of the police for showing a human face.

When Nigel's back was turned, Milton most improperly raised his glass to Lady Clark and mouthed 'Good Luck.' The grin he got in return made him wonder at Sir Nicholas's blind stupidity.

Chapter Twenty-one

Amiss had racked his brains all the way to the office that morning to turn up the name of someone who could tell him something about Nigel Clark. He drew a complete blank. He couldn't remember Nigel coming into the office more than once or twice. Then he recalled that Sir Nicholas had once got him a vacation job in the department—in the days before the unions stopped the employment of temporary clerical staff. Yes, of course. It had been the summer before Amiss became Sir Nicholas's Private Secretary, and he had heard about it when the union decision became known. Fulminations: the service now dominated by the whims of a crowd of oafs who should be employed digging ditches instead of dealing with papers they couldn't read without moving their lips.

Amiss couldn't think of any unofficial way of finding out where Nigel had worked. He didn't have any contacts in Personnel Division, bar his Careers Advisor, with whom his relations had been, of necessity, above-board and rather formal. He still remembered the interview there when he was informed of the privilege that was to be his in working for Sir Nicholas. Not a hint, amid all the piety, that he was known to his staff, with reason, as 'Old Nick'. No—string-pulling with Personnel Division was out. He referred the problem to his subconscious and walked into his office hoping for a day of peace unmarked by any more murderous assaults on public servants.

Personnel Division had obviously worked at lightning speed to find a replacement for Gladys. Others could wait for months for urgent clerical staff, but perish the thought that a Permanent Secretary might be inconvenienced for a moment—even a stand-in Permanent Secretary. Poor Gladys's desk was manned by a familiar figure, feet in the in-tray, gnawing on one of the canteen's polystyrene rolls and gazing at the generous breasts of a pouting young woman, which tumbled over half of page three of his newspaper.

'Hey, Robert, cop a load of this pair. They're fantastic.'

'What are you doing here, you sex-crazed yob?' asked Amiss with pleasure.

'That old tart in Personnel rung me up and said as how there was a National Emergency and my place was by your side.'

Amiss was amazed at the intelligence the old tart had displayed in sending him someone who knew the job. Phil had been the bright spot of the office until Sir Nicholas had him ejected on the famous occasion when he overheard himself being referred to as 'Shit-face'. Gladys had been in all respects an unworthy successor.

'Well, if it wouldn't swell your already enormous head, I'd say I was pleased to see you back.'

'Up yours,' said Phil affably, and returned to his studies.

Amiss got himself a cup of coffee and fell on the more sober newspapers. Even *The Times* had brought itself to make Gladys's murder the lead story. The report was heavy with references to grave concern in Whitehall and embarrassing implications for the government. One of the popular papers had heard rumours of a vendetta against Sir Nicholas and his staff. At least Milton would be relieved that they hadn't discovered who was on the short-list of suspects.

'Swap?' asked Phil, who read *The Times* as enthusiastically as his tabloid. (It was generally thought that the ghastly rag he claimed to love was just another tactic in his *épater le bourgeois* campaign—or 'stickin' it up their noses', as he would more likely put it.)

Amiss leafed listlessly through Phil's paper. Even the news of an alleged rapist vicar failed to arouse his interest.

'Don't you want to hear about the murders?'

'Nah. Julia's already told me about 'em. Seems to me everyone's making too much of a bleedin' fuss about two ole geezers that should of been buried years ago.'

Phil's iconoclasm wasn't usually too much for Amiss, but decency required him to remonstrate.

'For Christ's sake, Phil. I agree about Sir Nicholas but it's a bit thick about Gladys.'

'From all I've 'eard the old bint didn't enjoy life much,' said Phil carelessly. 'Seems to me the murderer was doin' 'er a favour.' And he bent to a consideration of *The Times*'s leading article on Israel and the Left Bank.

Amiss gave up. There was no point in trying to impose even the most widely held social *convenances* on Phil. It only made him more outrageous. Anyway, he didn't want to be called 'a pompous git'. It was something he secretly worried he might become if he stayed in the civil service long enough. Phil had a way of touching the nerve.

'I fink them Palestinians should kick the Israelis in the arse,' said Phil consideringly. 'Seems to me the latest carry-on over the …'

Amiss cut him short, cursing, not for the first time, the respect for Phil's intelligence which had made him propel the latter towards evening classes and an interest in current affairs. There didn't seem to be a clerical assistant's job in Whitehall busy enough to engage Phil for a full day's work. He read the newspapers with more attention than his more elevated colleagues and liked nothing better than embarrassing them by showing that he was more up-to-date and better informed than they. Amiss shuddered at the recollection of the time Phil had become converted to monetarism, and had proved in argument to have a grasp of the views of Milton Friedman which made mincemeat of his own vaguely-held Keynesianism.

'Get on with some work.'

'Don't want an argument, do you?' said Phil, who always saw through attempts to kill off debates. 'O.K. then, I'll leave you in peace. But I ain't got no work to do. I done it all before you got in, you lazy bugger.'

Amiss retired to his paper work in a dignified silence. Julia had gone off to find more audiences for her story, and George and Bernard seemed disinclined for chat.

'That's a good picture of that poofdah,' broke in Phil, who had the habit of assuming that one could instantly divine the subject he was alluding to. 'Untrained mind,' said some. Amiss had seen too many people wrong-footed by the technique to believe it was entirely unconscious.

'Which poofdah?'

'That Nigel Clark. There's a picture in 'ere of 'im and 'is mum, lookin' all sad. That's a laugh. Imagine anyone looking sad about that ole fart gettin' done in.'

'What are you talking about? You don't know Nigel Clark.'

'Yes, I do,' said Phil aggrievedly. 'Worked with 'im in Accounts Division, didn't I, when he was doin' a few weeks graft eighteen months ago?'

Amiss couldn't believe his luck. An unsolicited piece of information at last.

'What do you mean, poofdah?'

'Bum bandit. Queen. Fag. Gay. 'Omosexual. What do you think I mean?'

Amiss resisted the temptation to thump him. He could do that later—when he had extracted whatever Phil had on offer.

'I mean what makes you think he's a poofdah, you narg?'

'I 'aven't got where I am today wivout bein' able to spot a poofdah when I see one. Besides, I used to listen to 'im on the phone talkin' to 'is poofdah friends. 'Eard 'im cooin' down the phone at some feller called Billy makin' dates to go dancin' in one of them gay discos up West.'

'Sir Nicholas can't have liked that much.'

'Nigey baby seemed to be keepin' it pretty quiet from what I could hear of his arrangements. 'E never knew I was listenin'. Didn't realize how good my ears are,' said Phil modestly.

'You should have been a detective, you nosey little bugger.'

'The only pigs I want anyfink to do with are the ones I eat for breakfast,' said Phil, turning over to the Business News. The conversation clearly was closed.

Amiss let ten minutes go by before slipping out to find a private telephone. He wasn't going to risk using the extension in the next office with Phil around. Mrs Milton wasn't in, he was informed by a helpful secretary, but he might try just before lunch. He swore to himself. There was no point in trying Milton. He had said he wouldn't be in all morning. Nigel would have to wait his turn.

Later in the morning, Sanders called for Amiss to discuss the brief for the Secretary of State's Question Time in the House the following day. 'Have the police been back?' he asked, as Amiss rose to leave.

'No. They said last night they'd finished with the room.'

'Oh, well, in that case I'll move back in this afternoon. And, by the way, would you mind sorting out Sir Nicholas's private papers? I think you'd know your way around them better than I should. Use your own discretion about what should be destroyed.'

There was still no Mrs Milton. Amiss went back to his office and decided he might as well deal with Sir Nicholas's papers before lunch. He worked quickly through the desk drawers. Everything there that Sanders wouldn't need could be chucked out. Then he turned his attentions to the small cabinet with the combination lock in which were kept all confidential papers.

As he had expected, there was very little there. Sir Nicholas didn't hold on to departmental papers. He either took them home with him or sent them back for Amiss to deal with. Amiss leafed through the solitary folder marked 'Personal'. It consisted mainly of neat accounts of personal expenditure incurred while travelling on departmental business. There was a small batch of receipts from restaurants which Sir Nicholas used for official entertaining. Amiss wondered idly why he locked up innocuous stuff like this. Still, it was in character. He had even insisted that his staff lock up the departmental telephone directories at night on the grounds that they were confidential. Amiss supposed that it would be proper procedure to send in a claim for these expenses to the Accounts Division, asking them to forward the cheque to Lady Clark. Perhaps he had better ask Sanders if he thought it would be too tactless. Probably depended on how much money was involved.

He was flicking through the receipts to estimate the amount to be claimed when he came on one headed:

J. RITCHIE
CONFIDENTIAL INVESTIGATIONS

Dated a week previously, it recorded that the bill of £300 for professional services had been paid in full. Amiss stood for a moment thinking. He put his head through the connecting door and saw that Phil had disappeared. He went back into Sir Nicholas's room and rang Milton's office.

Wednesday Afternoon

Chapter Twenty-two

Milton was in a rage, as much with himself for failing to make a simple routine check, as with the P.C. involved, who had been one of those investigating the Monday lunchtime movements of all the staff in Embankment Tower, government employees or otherwise (the building housed a number of unrelated enterprises).

'Why in Christ's name didn't he let us know the minute he found out that Nigel Clark worked in that building?' he yelled at Romford.

'I suppose he thought we'd know.'

'And why didn't we?'

'Because no one told us,' said Romford reasonably.

Milton's fairmindedness reasserted itself. Romford was right. It was more his own fault than anyone else's; he had made an unwarranted assumption: tight security would have stopped any outsiders getting through the net unobserved, true, but why had he blindly categorized Nigel Clark as such an outsider? The rawest recruit, given the opportunity Milton had had, would have asked Nigel about his movements on Monday—a matter of routine, whether or not the hypothetical investigator had known that Embankment Tower housed other enterprises besides offshoots of government.

'Seems a bit odd, sir, that he didn't mention it to you this morning.'

Are you rubbing my nose in it, Romford? 'It does indeed. He doesn't have an alibi, and he must have known that if I knew where he worked I'd have questioned him about what he was doing. That young man is going to regret being shifty with me. Ring him up and tell him I want to see him here at 4.00 this afternoon. I should be finished with Jenkins well before that. Don't accept any excuses, but don't put the wind up him. You know how to handle it.'

He returned to his papers, still fuming with himself. He wondered glumly how he was going to explain it away to the Assistant Commissioner. It wouldn't be easily forgiven if he didn't come up with a murderer pretty quickly.

It was one o'clock—time he sent out for a sandwich. No, better make it two. He wouldn't be eating until late that evening. Oh, Christ, it would be curry again. This was getting beyond a joke. Surely it wasn't impossible to think of an alternative unfashionable restaurant with dim lighting and foreign waiters.

Ten minutes later, he was biting into a soggy salad sandwich when his telephone rang.

'May I speak to Superintendent Milton, please? It's Robert Amiss here from the Department of Conservation.'

'Good Lord, Robert. Aren't you breaking cover?'

'No, Jim. I've found something I can tell you about formally, for once. As you're obviously alone, however, I'll be able to pass on as well the illicit information I've been trying to speak to your wife about this morning.'

Amiss was brief and to the point. J. Ritchie's confidential investigations came as a bombshell to Milton. 'Where did you find this?' he choked, when he had taken details.

'In the security cabinet in Sir Nicholas's room.'

'But we checked that. There was nothing of any importance in it.'

'I'm sorry, Jim, but you overlooked this.'

Milton's humiliation was complete. 'That's the second bloomer I've made already on this case. I must be getting past it.'

'Don't blame yourself, Jim. The receipt was buried in a pile of restaurant bills. I wouldn't have spotted it if I hadn't had a reason to go through them one by one.'

Milton wasn't much cheered up. 'What's your other information? Did we miss a signed confession lying on the floor beside the corpse?'

Amiss told him what Phil had said about Nigel's sexual proclivities. Milton toyed with the idea of blaming himself for not guessing that morning, but decided he had had enough self-flagellation for one afternoon.

'It does give Nigel a possible motive, doesn't it, Jim? Sir Nicholas would have gone wild if he had found out about this. He was incredibly bigoted about gays. Called them queers and believed they should all be locked up. Have you found out anything more about where Nigel was Monday lunchtime?'

'I have indeed. Would you believe that he was in the building? He's worked there for the last three months. He's employed by a computer services company—they lease the tenth floor.'

'Does he have an alibi?'

'We don't think so. No one from his office saw him around during the period we're interested in. The constable who was checking the movements of the tenth-floor staff hadn't been able to get hold of him. He hasn't been to work since his mother rang him with the news on Monday afternoon, and his home telephone wasn't being answered.'

'Won't he be with his mother?'

'He is. I talked to him at her house this morning. The first bloomer I mentioned was that when I saw him I didn't know where he worked and didn't ask. I've been kicking myself about that for the last half-hour.'

Amiss muttered sympathies and rang off. He felt thankful that he was working in a job where a minor cock-up didn't usually threaten one's career. Milton would be in deep trouble if it emerged that Nigel was the double murderer. There were those who would blame the police for Gladys's death.

He spent the time before Sanders's arrival dealing with routine paper work with an attention to detail which was uncharacteristic of him. Normally the polished pointlessness of most of the prose he had to read led him to skim it at maximum speed. At present, though, he couldn't afford any lapses which might draw attention to his preoccupation with the murders. The civil service expected its staff to work normally, whatever was happening around them. It didn't matter if your wife was having a baby, the government had fallen, there was a threatened war or your clerical assistant had been murdered. Your job was to maintain an impassive exterior and carry on as usual; displays of emotion made you suspect. Amiss had a mental image of the kind of bureaucracy which would emerge in the bunkers after a nuclear holocaust. He could see the surviving civil servants sitting round drafting and redrafting emergency instructions, with as fine an attention as ever to detached prose and literate wording.

Phil had been despatched for sandwiches. He returned, grumbling about being 'a bloody body-servant'. Amiss enquired politely if the pressure of work was too much for him.

'There's sod-all to do. I've spent an hour looking for the appointments diary. Can't find it anywhere. Do you fink they're burying it wiv Gladys so she can carry it into the next world?'

'It's probably in Sanders's office.'

'I've looked.'

'Well, it'll turn up,' said Amiss absently. 'It's probably been stuffed in a drawer.' His mind had gone back to Nigel Clark. He could hardly wait to hear how Milton's interview with him went. He didn't know how he could get through the afternoon meetings when all he could think about was what Milton would have to tell him that night.

Chapter Twenty-three

Milton had better things to do than think about the evening. He was on his way to see J. Ritchie. This meant yet another alteration to his time-table. Jenkins and Nigel Clark had each had to be postponed by an hour, and Alf Shaw, who had already been put off twice, had agreed rather peevishly to be interviewed the following morning. He couldn't manage the early evening.

Milton wondered if he wasn't making a mistake in insisting on seeing all the principals himself. He could have used one of his inspectors for Ritchie and Shaw. But he was stubbornly convinced still that only by seeing all these people himself could he build up the picture of Sir Nicholas which was essential to understanding why he was murdered. He'd better be right. The Assistant Commissioner had said a few ominous words about the time he was taking to see everyone concerned. Milton had had to fudge the issue of why he had been apparently knocking off work at between eight and nine o'clock every evening. The A.C. would have been happier if he could point to a record of activity going on to midnight, he thought sourly. He had been only partially mollified by Milton's excuse—that he was spending his late evenings going over the day's evidence and devising his questions for the next day's interviews. The A.C. had admitted grudgingly that this policy had paid off and that Milton's homework and intuition seemed to be having unexpectedly good results.

Ritchie's office was rather less squalid than Milton had expected. He was obviously a rather up-market private detective.

He inhabited a small set of rooms in a slightly decaying Edwardian office block in Kensington. But, if a trifle shabby, they were at least clean and comfortable. Ritchie himself was a tall, bland young man, dressed in the jeans, sweater and particoloured crepe-soled shoes that constituted the work, weekend and evening dress of the young Kensington male.

He looked vaguely familiar. As Milton introduced himself and sat down he became convinced he had seen Ritchie before—wearing a rather more formal outfit. Ritchie smiled.

'You won't remember me, Superintendent, but I was briefly a C.I.D. sergeant when you were an inspector working on the Rutland Square murders.'

Milton wondered if Ritchie was another disgraced copper setting himself up in the only trade he knew. No, he couldn't be. Sackings were so rare at the Yard that the people involved became a nine days' wonder. He now remembered Ritchie slightly as an unremarkable but reasonably efficient officer.

'You left about five years ago, then?'

'Four, actually. I couldn't stand it any more. I've never enjoyed having to say "Yes, sir" and "No, sir". And besides, there wasn't much money to be made in the police force. I set up on my own with my gratuity and I'm making twice as much now as I'd be making as an inspector.'

Milton decided he didn't like him. Too bloody cocky. He didn't like private detectives at the best of times. Most of them made their money out of that very messing with people's private lives that caused Milton his occasional bouts of self-disgust.

He forced a smile. 'I'm glad things have worked out well for you.'

'Thanks. I've been luckier than I expected. You'd have thought that the liberalizing of the divorce laws would have spoiled the market, but you'd be amazed how many people still prefer the good old-fashioned contested divorce with mud being flung in all directions. There are enough suspicious wives in Kensington to keep me in work for years.'

'Well, as I told you on the telephone, I've come to find out what work you've been doing for Sir Nicholas Clark, who, I suppose, was a suspicious husband.'

'And father,' laughed Ritchie.

'Father?'

'Yeah. He had me trailing the two of them.'

'Can you tell me about it from the beginning?'

'O.K. I don't mind breaking confidentiality to help the course of justice.'

Milton thought Ritchie would be more likely to break it for the good of his wallet. 'If you're that keen, why did you wait for us to find you?'

Ritchie looked embarrassed. 'Oh, yeah. Fair point. But I didn't see anything in the paper about the wife or son having been around when he was murdered, so I thought my info would be irrelevant.'

'Hmmm,' said Milton. 'Well, I'll give you the benefit of the doubt if you cooperate fully now. I'm sure you'll recognize the value of maintaining good relations with the police.'

'Oh, certainly,' said Ritchie. 'Here goes. He was a funny fellow, Sir Nicholas. Rang me up out of the blue. Said he'd got my number from the yellow pages. Started by asking me if I was one of those seedy little fellows in a dirty mac who could be spotted a mile away by anyone they were trailing. I had to use my poshest accent to convince him he wouldn't be soiling himself by employing me.'

'Did you meet?'

'No. It was all done by phone and post. He sent me photographs and said he'd ring me in a few days to check progress.'

'When did he first approach you?'

Ritchie consulted his diary. 'The Wednesday before last.'

'You must have worked fast to have had your bill in and paid last week.'

'I did. It only took a couple of days. I was able to give him the goods on the two of them when he rang me last Monday week. It was all very easy. I trailed the wife first, and, as luck would have it, spotted her holding hands with a fellow over dinner in a secluded restaurant. Followed him home after that and was waiting outside the next morning when he went off to work. It was easy to get his name. When he had gone into his office building I just asked the doorman who he was. Said I thought he was familiar looking. Sir Nicholas got a nasty shock when I told him his wife was all lovey-dovey with Martin Jenkins. I didn't think there were still people around who used words like "gutter-snipe".'

'He didn't want you to find out if they were having an affair?'

'No. I offered to go on trailing her in the hope of getting some real dirt—hotel registers and that sort of thing. But he didn't seem interested. I thought that was funny. I'd assumed he was looking for divorce evidence.'

'What about Nigel?'

'That was easy, too. Sir Nicholas was at home on the Friday night, so I knew his missus wouldn't be likely to sneak off again. I followed Nigel instead. Landed up at a gay pub off the Charing Cross Road. Young Nigel spent most of the evening gazing into the eyes of a big butch guy. Saw them kissing once. I followed his boyfriend home and got his address. Then all I had to do was wait till Monday and ring up my mate in the Post Office who helps me out sometimes and ask him to get me the name of the subscriber who lived there. Ronald Maitland, it was. Sir Nicholas seemed to recognize that name too.'

'Do you think he had suspected that Nigel was involved with a man?'

'I suppose so. All he had asked me to do was to find out where Nigel went in the evenings and who he was socializing with. When he heard he'd been kissing Maitland he didn't want me to do any more work for him. Said he'd got all he wanted, and would I send in the bill.'

'Three hundred pounds seems a bit high for the amount of work you did.'

Ritchie was confident enough by now to let a smirk pass over his face.

'Look, he was loaded. Big house, big job. I always double my charges at least when I've got a client who's rolling in it. They don't often complain. They're always a bit ashamed of hiring a private dick anyway, and they don't want to demean themselves any further by quibbling about money. He paid up like a lamb by return of post. Just as well, considering what's happened to him. It'd be a bit embarrassing to ask his family to pay up.'

That was enough for Milton. He couldn't stand another minute of this revolting creep. He gritted his teeth, said a polite goodbye and headed off to meet one of Ritchie's victims.

Chapter Twenty-four

Martin Jenkins was sitting behind a cluttered desk in a modest room in his headquarters. It looked as if he lived up to his egalitarian principles—in public at least. Milton wondered how he would cope with a rich wife. He couldn't quite see this scrawny individual, who seemed to have several buttons missing from his chain-store suit, sitting in Lady Clark's drawing-room. Still, it was amazing how you could get used to money. Milton had himself always had pretty simple tastes, but Ann's large income made it surprisingly easy to develop a liking for decent wine, expensive holidays and good restaurants. He remembered the curry house and shuddered apprehensively. How many years was it since he'd regarded a third-class meal in an Indian restaurant as a treat to be looked forward to? Did Jenkins starve himself, or was a high metabolic rate concomitant with the fire of conviction in his Welsh belly?

'Sit down, Superintendent.'

'Thank you, sir. I'm sorry that I had to postpone our appointment.'

'That's quite all right, Superintendent. I understand the pressures you must be operating under.'

Milton felt buoyed up by this unexpectedly polite reception from the scourge of the police force. The soft Welsh voice went on. 'I know what you've come to talk to me about. I've heard from Eleanor.'

'I hope Lady Clark wasn't too upset about having to answer questions about her relationship with you.'

'No, she wasn't, Superintendent. I must admit that I was furious when she first told me about it. I was thinking of lodging a complaint about your intrusiveness, but Eleanor talked me round. She said you'd been very apologetic about the whole business and that it would be better for me to cooperate.'

Good for Lady Clark. Love's turned this one soft. 'Lady Clark has told me about how you got involved with each other, sir, and that she was going to move in with you. What I need to know is: first, what your relationship with Sir Nicholas was like generally, and second, whether you know if he had any idea you were having an affair with his wife.'

'I didn't have a relationship with Sir Nicholas. I met him only a few times—after I'd got to know Eleanor. It's not easy meeting a man you're cuckolding. I went out of my way to avoid talking to him. Where I come from, what I was doing was something to be ashamed of, and, though I couldn't regret my affair with Eleanor, my Methodist background made me feel embarrassed every time I caught sight of her husband.'

'Apart from the embarrassment, how did you feel about him, sir?'

'I disliked him, of course. He represented everything I distrust most in our society. He had sold out to the Establishment and seemed to be using his position to block every proposal the Left ever put up to his department for increasing employment in the recycling industry.'

'But surely that was a matter for his Secretary of State rather than Sir Nicholas himself?'

'Come now, Superintendent. I know who runs this country. Poor old Harvey Nixon is completely in the hands of his civil servants. All he ever did was sign or read out the decisions Sir Nicholas fed him.'

'Lady Clark has presumably told you what happened over Mr Nixon's speech at the Monday morning meeting.'

'Yes. It made me sick, but I wasn't really surprised. Harvey isn't a fool. He might not be up to the job, but he does his homework all right. I knew there was something peculiar about his performance that morning, and I felt sorry for him. I may be a critic of the government's flabbiness, but I couldn't take any pleasure in seeing one of its most decent members reduced to that state.'

'I understand that he had to give the speech at short notice because Sir Nicholas said the TUC were going to make an issue of it.'

'He made that up. There wasn't anything in that paper that would have caused a row in the normal course of events. It's a very uncontroversial area of the department's work.'

'I thought that was the case, sir, but it's useful to have it confirmed.'

'Clark must have had a brainstorm. Any idiot could see he was jeopardizing his own career, playing a vicious trick like that.'

'We are still puzzled by his behaviour, sir. I've rarely come across a stranger personality. What was your view of him as a human being?—ideologies apart.'

'My direct contact with him was too limited for me to get beyond my initial dislike for his reserve. They're not a very warm-blooded lot, these officials, but he was the coldest fish I ever came across. He didn't seem ever to loosen up. I used to observe him covertly when he attended meetings with Harvey. He sat behind him and, of course, never said anything. Just used to pass Harvey the occasional note; otherwise he just sat there, superciliously. I think the only time I ever saw him smile was when Harvey had fumbled his way through the first part of that disastrous speech. I didn't know then what he was finding so funny, but I suppose we know now.'

'But you must have got to know quite a lot about him from Lady Clark?'

'Eleanor and I talked about all sorts of things, Superintendent, but we kept off the subject of her husband as much as possible. I knew they were unhappy, of course, and she told me how their relationship had changed over the years, but what she needed was to enjoy the time we had together. She was like a kid let out of school. Full of enjoyment of the simplest pleasures. I don't think she's had any fun for years.'

'But she did have a very close relationship with her son, sir.'

'I don't know much about that.' Jenkins was abrupt. 'He hasn't been home much during the past few years, so she'd had to learn to do without him most of the time.'

Milton bet that Jenkins was holding out on him about Nigel. Should he probe further? No, it wasn't worth it. Jenkins would hit the roof if Milton even implied that Nigel was gay, though Milton was morally certain that Lady Clark must have known, and told Jenkins. No, in all decency, that was something to talk to Nigel about first. It was a thin enough motive for murdering his father.

'You had no reason to suppose that Sir Nicholas knew about you and Lady Clark?'

'Not until Monday,' said Jenkins evenly. 'Then I knew that he did.'

'What happened, sir?'

'He caught up with me as we left the conference room and whispered that he wanted to see me in the corridor outside to discuss my seduction of his wife.'

'What did you say, sir?'

'What could I say? I was afraid of a public scene if I didn't agree to talk to him outside. I was just about to go out with him there and then when Alf Shaw called me over. When I looked for him later I couldn't see him anywhere.'

'You must have been very disconcerted, sir.'

'Disconcerted is not the word, Superintendent. I had faced up to the fact that it would probably be very difficult when Eleanor at last told him she was leaving, but I had thought that at least things could be worked out in a reasonably civilized way. I was prepared to resign from the Industry and Government Group to avoid embarrassing him. I didn't think he really cared about Eleanor, so I hoped we'd get away with it without any great traumas.'

'How did he seem when he spoke to you, sir?'

'I find it very difficult to describe, Superintendent. He wasn't threatening or anything—no fisticuffs in prospect. He didn't even look angry or upset. He almost seemed pleased with himself.'

'He hadn't said anything to Lady Clark about you?'

'No. She'd have told me, of course, as I'd have told her about this if it hadn't been for the murder. When that happened I decided to keep this quiet for fear of worrying her, though I can't really see how anyone could think it gives me a motive for murder. Nothing he could have said would have stopped me from taking Eleanor away. I wasn't afraid of anything worse than embarrassment when I went out to look for him. I was mainly anxious to know how the hell he knew about us.'

'I can tell you, sir,' said Milton, and he briefly summarized Ritchie's role in enlightening Sir Nicholas.

Jenkins seemed amazed. 'That means he must have been harbouring suspicions beforehand. I can't imagine how. Eleanor's very good at hiding her feelings—she's had plenty of practice at it—and we were always very careful to meet when he was at work or away.'

'Maybe he paid more attention to her than you supposed.'

'Maybe he did. Though that doesn't fit in with the way he treated her. She says that most evenings he didn't spend more than half an hour with her.'

'There are many things about Sir Nicholas that are still puzzling me,' said Milton, 'and I doubt if we are ever going to understand exactly why he acted as he did in the period leading up to his murder.'

'Is there anything else you need to know from me, Superintendent?'

'No, thank you, sir. I won't take up any more of your time. I'm grateful for your cooperation.'

He seemed to be producing that policeman's cliché rather often, thought Milton as he left Jenkins. It wasn't often that suspects spilled the beans with such willingness as most had on this case. Then again, it wasn't often that policemen were as well briefed as he had been by Amiss. He grinned as he thought about his elegant new recruit to the ranks of coppers' narks. He was a far cry from Milton's last experience of that breed—a slimy little creature with a battered dripping nose, an insatiable appetite for ten-pound notes and a line in misleading information which had led Milton to give him up as a bad job. He would be sorry to lose touch with Amiss when this was all over.

He looked at his watch. It was almost five o'clock. Too near rush hour to take a taxi back to the Yard. He'd be better off on the tube. He noticed with grim amusement that a young man standing beside him in the packed carriage was wearing a badge saying 'Glad to be Gay'. Well, he didn't suppose Nigel Clark had had reason to be very glad about it. He sure as hell wasn't going to be glad about anything very much when Milton had finished with him.

Chapter Twenty-five

'You were less than honest with me this morning, sir.'

Nigel Clark looked as frightened as Milton had hoped he would. 'I answered all your questions, Superintendent.'

'You must have known that it was relevant that you had no alibi for the time when your father was killed.'

'Well, I admit it was a relief that you didn't say anything about it. I assumed that meant you knew who the murderer was.'

'You know perfectly well that I wouldn't have been wasting my time with you if I knew any such thing.'

'I can't be expected to know how the police operate,' replied Clark with a sudden flash of spirit.

'I am in no mood for silly arguments. I should like your comments on the fact that you had the opportunity to kill your father and that your alibi for the murder of Mrs Bradley is substantiated only by your mother.'

He thought for a moment that this brutality was going to precipitate a breakdown, but Nigel Clark was made of better stuff than that.

'Why the hell should I kill my father and a woman I had never met before?' he asked defiantly.

'Possibly, sir, because your father had found out that you were emotionally involved with Ronald Maitland, and Mrs Bradley had heard you and Sir Nicholas arguing about it before you murdered him.'

That did it. Milton thought for a moment that Nigel was going to be sick. He sat frigid and pale in his chair for several moments and then whispered 'How did you find out?'

'I am under no obligation to reveal my sources, sir. You, however, are under an obligation to tell me the truth. I may tell you that your evasiveness has put you in a serious position. I could arrest you immediately on suspicion of both murders if I so chose. I warn you also that I shall check every statement you make with the utmost care. If I find you have told me any lies or have concealed any information relevant to either murder, I shall be obliged to take a most serious view. In your own interests I advise you to tell me honestly about your relationship with your father, particularly in recent weeks, and what occurred when you saw him just before he was murdered.'

Milton was taking a risk. He knew perfectly well that no one would authorize the arrest of Nigel Clark when his alibi for Gladys's murder was backed up by his mother. At least, not until there was a great deal more to go on than there was at present. Nor was there a shred of positive evidence that Nigel had seen Sir Nicholas that Monday lunchtime. Still, he was in no position to call the bluff of a policeman who had revealed himself to be a tough nut. Milton set his face in what he hoped was a threatening expression and waited.

'I don't know where to begin.'

'Take it chronologically, sir. Tell me about your relationship with your father.'

'I was sorry for him.'

Milton looked at Nigel blankly. It was the first time he had heard Sir Nicholas represented as an object of pity.

'Why?'

'Because I couldn't love him, I suppose, and I thought he desperately wanted me to.'

'And why couldn't you love him?'

'Because he made me feel a failure. All through my school and university days I felt I was letting him down every time he read a school report or heard the results of one of my exams. He never said much directly when he was upset. He would just retreat to his study for several hours. Then he'd come out and tell me he was going to arrange more private tuition for me since I was obviously being badly taught. I was never any good, though. I could never do more than scrape a pass in the subjects he really cared about and he wasn't impressed by what I managed to achieve in Maths and Science. He always talked about scientists as if they were some race of illiterate technicians.'

'I still don't see why this should have made you sorry for him. Surely you were resentful?'

'Sometimes I was, but I didn't think he could help himself. He wanted me to be like him, you see, and I was so different that he was constantly disappointed. I was so nervous of adding to that disappointment by appearing stupid in conversation that I avoided him as much as possible. Sometimes if we were together for a while and I made an excuse to leave he'd say something like "Of course I realize you've got better things to do" in a way which made me think he was hurt. But I couldn't help wanting to get away. I couldn't cope.'

'You were close to your mother?'

'Yes, very. And that made it worse. I think he was upset every time he saw us laughing over something, or talking about some book we had both read. We used to go to the cinema together when I was a kid. He wouldn't come with us because he despised films, and after a while we didn't invite him any more. He'd just stay at home by himself. He must have felt that he was an outsider.'

'Did things improve after you went to university?'

'No. If anything, they got worse. I rarely brought my friends home because he made them feel so ill-at-ease, and he seemed insulted when I went to stay with them rather than be at home.'

'It must have been a great strain for you to live in the same house with him.'

'Yes, it was. I couldn't wait to leave, though I was sorry to leave my mother on her own with him.'

Ah, thought Milton. *So she didn't tell him about Jenkins. Or is he covering up?* 'What about your involvement with Ronald Maitland?'

Nigel Clark looked embarrassed. Then he looked Milton straight in the eye. 'I'm in love with him.'

'Is this recent?'

'It's been going on for about three months. I met him at a disco.'

'A gay disco?'

'Yes. I've known for three years that I was gay. That was another reason I didn't want to bring my friends home. I knew what my father thought of people like us.'

'Did your mother know?'

'Yes, she did. I told her quite a long time ago, and she has met Ronald. The three of us had lunch together last month when we had decided to live together.'

'How did she take it?'

'Very well. Mothers seem to come to terms with it much easier than fathers, if my friends' experiences are anything to go by. She was really quite relieved about Ronald. She thought I'd be better off settled down. She didn't like me being promiscuous.'

'Were you going to tell your father?'

'No. Mother and I talked about it and decided not to say anything. We thought he might realize it himself eventually. We couldn't see any point in precipitating a row.'

'You never suspected he might know what you were? He didn't remark for instance on the absence of girlfriends?'

'Well, I used to pretend often that I was going out with a girl when in fact it was a bloke. He never made any comments or asked any questions about my sex life.'

'When did he tell you that he knew?' asked Milton, hoping his gamble had paid off.

'He rang me at the office last Monday morning about 10.30.'

After abandoning poor old Nixon, thought Milton.

'He said he had heard something very disturbing about my private life and wished to talk to me about it after the meeting.

He asked me to come up and wait for him in one of the nearby rooms at about 12.30.'

'He said nothing else?'

'No. Just enough to leave me worried.'

'Did you tell anyone about this?'

'Not then. I couldn't talk freely on the office phone.'

'So you went up there at 12.30?'

'Yes. He came in a few minutes later and told me that he knew all about Ronald and me. He called me a pervert.'

'What did you do?'

'I broke down, I'm afraid. I couldn't take it. He made me feel sordid.'

'What did you say to him?'

'I couldn't speak for a couple of minutes. He stood there watching me and then said something about never having expected to father a queer. I shouted at him then. I hardly know what I said. Just something about finding love at last with a better man than he was. Then I ran.'

'Where did you go?'

'Out of the building. I didn't come back for about an hour. I just walked round and round Westminster aimlessly. I hadn't been long back when I got the news that he was dead.'

'You must have hated him when he said those things to you.'

'In a way. And yet, Superintendent, and I know you're not going to find this easy to believe, I still felt sorry for him. I almost thought he was envious of me for being in love.'

'You didn't follow him into the lavatory and kill him?'

'I did not.'

'Did you see any sign of Mrs Bradley?'

'No, I didn't. But I was so upset that she could have been in the room half the time and I wouldn't have known.'

'Did your mother know about this episode?'

'Yes. I told her on Monday afternoon.'

So Lady Clark hadn't been as frank as she might have been, either. Well, she could hardly be blamed for that. Milton remembered Ann's words about mother-love. Was it conceivable that he had in fact confided to his mother that he had killed his father and that they had together hatched a conspiracy to kill Gladys at the first available opportunity? If so, how could they know they would find her alone? Or were they just relying on luck? Milton tried to imagine Lady Clark standing by while her beloved son knifed Gladys. He couldn't.

He let Nigel go. There was nothing more to be extracted from him for the moment. He sat down to think about where he should go from here. He had seen all the possibles except Alf Shaw, and he couldn't really take him seriously as a suspect. What was he going to do now? Interview the lot of them all over again? Forget his kid gloves and try storm-trooper tactics this time? He wouldn't mind putting the screws on Wells, but he would have a great deal of trouble gearing himself up to bully people as pleasant as Nixon, Parkinson, Jenkins and Lady Clark. Maybe the A.C. should put someone else on the job. He might suggest that himself tomorrow morning. Admit to being awash with information which pointed in several ways at once—but always inconclusively. Wait a minute. He'd have to see Stafford about his weekend telephone call with Sir Nicholas and tax him with what Lady Clark had heard of it. His telephone interrupted this train of thought. Amiss was on the other end again. He sounded very formal.

'Superintendent Milton? Mr Sanders would be grateful if you could call over to see him. He has something to tell you that may be relevant to your enquiries.'

Wednesday Evening

Chapter Twenty-six

As Milton hurried over to the Department of Conservation, he was speculating furiously about what Sanders could possibly have found out. He hoped the meeting wasn't going to be a waste of time. Odds were that Sanders had just found out independently some relevant information which he couldn't know Amiss had already passed on to the police. Milton could do without having to go through with any such charade; he was feeling badly in need of some time to himself to reflect calmly on the case. He had been rushing from interview to paper work to interview, never having long enough without interruption to look at the evidence as a whole. It was the feeling of having let it all get on top of him that had led to his momentary defeatism after Nigel Clark had left. Offer to give up the case to someone else? Damned if he would. If he couldn't crack it, with all the help he had had from Amiss and the personal knowledge he had built up of most of the suspects, then why should anyone else do better? Milton didn't suffer from over-confidence, but neither did he go in for false modesty. His chances of finding the murderer were as good as anyone else's. He wasn't going to relinquish voluntarily the most publicized case he had ever had. Instead he would find the time to go over the evidence piece by piece and try to fit it into a pattern. He would do that before seeing the Assistant Commissioner the next morning—even if he had to stay up all night. Maybe he and Amiss would have the opportunity that evening to review some of it together.

He was curious about Sanders. Although Amiss kept on insisting that Sir Nicholas was an exception, Milton couldn't help feeling some prejudice against senior civil servants in general and Permanent Secretaries—even temporary ones—in particular. They seemed to be at best an intellectually arrogant breed. Milton wasn't looking forward to being patronized by a first-rate mind.

Amiss came down to reception to collect Milton. They had time for only a couple of minutes of private conversation, in which Amiss was able to reassure him that this wouldn't be a wasted visit. Milton asked apprehensively about Sanders.

'I always found him pleasant,' said Amiss, 'but I hadn't quite realized how good he is at his job. I hope to Christ they have the sense to confirm him as Permanent Secretary when this is all over. He's not just the best kind of civil servant, he's a human being as well. I haven't forgotten how he reacted to Gladys's death. You'll find him a bit formal, of course, but that goes with the job. We don't, as you know, go in for hail-fellow-well-met back-slappers.' With that, he ushered Milton into Sanders's presence.

Sanders had snow-white hair topping a rather rubicund face; his dark suit was cut to conceal his round stomach. Milton thought that at less serious moments he would resemble a taller version of a Cheeryble brother. His present gravity couldn't entirely eradicate the pleasant connotations of the laughter lines around his mouth and eyes. Amiss introduced them and asked Sanders if he would like them to be left alone.

'No, Robert. This is an informal meeting and you might be able to shed some light on what we are about to discuss. After all, latterly you must have known Nicholas better than I did. Don't feel inhibited. This isn't the time to close ranks, so forget about discretion. In deciding to tell the Superintendent about this curious business with Wells, I've had to put personal feelings before my professional dislike of breaching confidentiality. You, I suggest, should do the same.'

Well, well. Another mole. Milton felt privileged indeed.

As they sat down he noticed that much in the office had changed since Sanders had taken over. Along the bookcase stretched a line of busts of the classical composers. The walls glowed with life. Sanders seemed to favour pictures full of richness and incident. Milton recognized Vermeer and Botticelli. And Lowry, for heaven's sake. Sanders obviously didn't share Sir Nicholas's distaste for the proletariat. On a table beside his desk was a pile of library books in transit—and Milton recognized them as novels. That was a heartening sign.

Sanders asked him some polite questions about the case, which gave Milton an opportunity to reinforce his obvious desire to be helpful.

'I've made quite a lot of progress, sir, but I can't say that I'm close to a solution. It's a bewildering world, yours. It hasn't been easy to disentangle motives. Anything you can do to help will be greatly appreciated.'

Sanders smiled. 'I sympathize with you, Superintendent. I wouldn't like to be an outsider trying to get information out of civil servants and politicians. I'll give you any help I can. I am very angry about Mrs Bradley's death—frankly far more upset than I was about Sir Nicholas's. The Secretary of State has told me about his behaviour and I have reason to know that he treated a number of people badly. There haven't been a lot of tears shed for him here. I think he had forgotten he was supposed to be a public servant rather than an unhappy man taking his personal disappointments out on those around him.'

Milton noticed with amusement that Amiss's mouth had dropped open. So Amiss was wrong in thinking he had these people taped. They could still produce surprises.

'Have you any idea, sir, why Sir Nicholas acted as he did?'

'No, Superintendent. I was never a personal friend of his, though we were colleagues for many years. He seemed in the early days to be a reasonable enough fellow to deal with. You could always rely on him to play a straight bat. There was never any doubt about his ability: he had it in him to reach the very top. But over the past four or five years I detected a rapid change in him. He turned extremely offensive to colleagues and began to be obstructive for the sake of it. He didn't let this side of him show to his superiors, though, so he still gained promotion to Permanent Secretary. I hoped then that he would be satisfied and that pleasure in his success might soften him. Unfortunately, it proved to be otherwise. He became increasingly difficult to work with—recently, almost impossible. Of course, as you might expect, he was far too wily to do anything that would lead to demotion or early retirement. Until last weekend he always played by the rules.'

'You don't have any idea who might have murdered him?'

'Not until now, Superintendent. I realize the Secretary of State must have been very sore with him, but I could never see a man of his gentle disposition responding to any provocation with violence. I don't know of anyone else present at that meeting who could have had reason to do more than dislike Nicholas. Except, I regret to say, our Parliamentary Under-Secretary of State, William Wells, who, I now find, had an excellent reason to feel the urge to strike him with the nearest blunt instrument. And he is a man at least capable of savage anger. I have seen him lose his temper on several occasions when he thought he was being thwarted.'

'Go on,' said Milton, leaning forward expectantly.

'Late this afternoon, returning from a meeting, I was rung up by a junior colleague, Alan Wilmot, who was in a state of panic. He had heard from one of our regional offices that an article had appeared in today's local paper, written by Wells and headed "LOCAL M.P. SAVES 3,000 JOBS", with the sub-heading, "How I did it".'

Milton looked puzzled.

'I had better explain the background of this to you. The nub of the matter is that in Wells's constituency there is an enormous plant which deals with chemical recycling. It is desperately important to the economic health of the area, once all the ancillary jobs and the knock-on effect are taken into account. After a couple of bad years it is threatened with immediate closure by its multinational parent company. We were asked to bail it out by the company's English management and unions, who claimed that its long-term prospects were good, and that it was in the public interest to provide twenty million pounds of government money to keep it going for another year until the market took an upturn. The parent company had agreed that they would keep the plant operating if this interest-free loan were made available; repayment was to be over the next ten years.'

'Twenty million pounds is a great deal of money, sir. I shouldn't have expected it to be a reasonable request from a private company.'

'Well, it was to be just a loan, and three thousand added to the unemployment register is a lot of people. The decision rested on whether the company really was viable and would survive and be able to repay the money. Wells, as you might imagine, was desperately anxious to save the company. His seat is a marginal one, and for him to be able to claim the credit for saving so many jobs would have virtually guaranteed his being successful in the General Election which cannot be far away. He fought very hard within the department, the party and the government to get agreement to the loan. His hopes were pretty high. Too high, really. The decision was always in doubt. I have reason to believe that he made some incautiously arrogant statements in his constituency about his ability to pull it off.'

'But I thought ministers as junior as Wells didn't have much power?'

'Quite right, Superintendent. They don't. Our Mr Wells, however, is one of those who believe that by the sheer exercise of aggression and energy you can accomplish anything. He lobbied extensively both within and without the department, and used every opportunity to try to embarrass the government into making the money available.'

'And he succeeded?'

'No, he didn't, Superintendent. That is the whole point. Wells's self-congratulatory article appeared on the very day a letter had been sent out to the company telling its management that the loan would not be forthcoming. In an effort to claim the maximum credit for himself in his constituency, Wells had jumped the gun and set himself up for the most tremendous fall.'

'How could he get it so wrong, sir?' asked Milton, bewildered. Wells hadn't struck him as being an idiot.

'Because, Superintendent, Nicholas told him it was safe to go ahead with the article.'

Chapter Twenty-seven

Milton had long since lost the capacity to be surprised at Sir Nicholas's malevolence, but he could still be astounded at his ingenuity.

'I'm sorry, sir. I can't believe I've understood you correctly. Are you saying that Wells didn't know Sir Nicholas had given him false information, and that he therefore let the article appear today? In that case, I don't see what it has got to do with Sir Nicholas's murder. Or are you saying Wells knew on Monday morning about the trick Sir Nicholas had played on him and therefore had a motive to kill him? In which case, why didn't he stop the article?'

'Wells knew all right. I haven't been able to get hold of him this evening, but his Private Secretary tells me that he heard Wells having an argument on the telephone on Monday afternoon with the editor of the newspaper in question. He was trying to withdraw his article.'

Milton was still lost. Weren't Private Secretaries supposed to be omniscient?

'Why didn't the Private Secretary tell you about this earlier, sir?'

'He didn't grasp what was going on. He hadn't seen the article Wells had sent in, and didn't realize that it announced that the loan had been granted. He just assumed Wells had had second thoughts about something in it.'

'But why couldn't Wells kill the article?'

'Because it was too late; the paper had already gone to bed. Besides, there's no knowing how explicit he was with the editor.

Knowing him, he'd have started with bully-boy tactics, and found it difficult to climb down later and admit that he'd been totally wrong-footed.'

'But for heaven's sake, sir, Wells would surely have told you about it?'

'He certainly should have, Superintendent, and I shall be very interested to hear why he didn't. There hasn't been a word from him about it. That's why I was so thunderstruck when I heard. I have no idea what he's playing at. He cancelled several meetings scheduled for today and didn't come in to the office. He pleaded personal reasons. We haven't been able to get hold of him anywhere.'

'Is he expected in tomorrow, sir?'

'He is, and he'll have a warm reception. Even our mild-mannered Secretary of State will be hopping mad over this.'

'So you are suggesting, sir, that Wells found out that Sir Nicholas had landed him in the mire and killed him in a fit of rage?'

'That is going much too far, Superintendent. I am merely suggesting that if Wells—as seems certain—found out on Monday morning that his upstaging of his colleagues was going to threaten his career he would have been extremely upset.'

'He's very ambitious, isn't he?'

'Exceptionally so, Superintendent.'

'It looks as though we shall have to wait until tomorrow to find out what has caused him to remain silent about this since Monday. In the meantime, could we talk about Sir Nicholas's motive for playing such a dirty trick? I gather he didn't like Wells, but this was something which would reflect on the government and the department as well.'

'It certainly will. We have two options. Either we ring the company in the morning and tell them to ignore our letter rejecting their request, or we tell them later that a minister—albeit a junior minister—had been so badly misled by colleagues in government that he has given totally wrong information to a newspaper. If we do the first, we gain some time at the expense of looking like fools. It will give the government a chance to reconsider the argument for lending the money, and they may be driven to giving in to avoid the political embarrassment of opting for the second course.'

'As a matter of curiosity, why did the decision go against making the loan?'

'Because on balance we are pretty sure the company will fold within the next couple of years whatever we do. We would be taking an unacceptable risk with taxpayers' money.'

'In that case, surely the decision won't be reversed?'

'It's too close to an election for that to be a certainty. The Cabinet have already taken a courageous decision once. With this new complication, they may well change their minds. There was only a small majority against the loan anyway.'

'When was the decision taken?'

'Last Friday. That was a stroke of luck for Nicholas. The Cabinet usually meets on Thursdays, but it met late on this occasion because the Prime Minister was out of the country for most of the week. That meant that Nicholas was able to tell Wells on Friday evening to go ahead with the article, knowing that he wouldn't hear about the true decision until the following Monday.'

'You seem very certain, sir, that Sir Nicholas told Wells to go ahead.'

'I'm guessing a little, but I'm pretty sure that is what happened. Wells's Private Secretary told me that Wells had made an appointment with Nicholas to see him when news came through of the Cabinet decision. Wells had written two alternative articles. The other was a justification of the decision to reject the loan. It fell back on platitudes about the effort he would be putting into pushing government to invest in job-creation schemes in other firms in the constituency. Nicholas summoned Wells in the late afternoon. He went off to see him carrying both articles and didn't come back to his office again.'

Milton knitted his brows. 'I thought civil servants wrote this kind of article for their ministers. Isn't there some kind of elaborate P.R. service which controls what is sent to the press?'

'There is, Superintendent, but Wells insisted on writing the articles himself. Nicholas had undertaken to vet them for publication—another proof that he was trying to make mischief. From what Alan Wilmot has told me about the article which has appeared, no civil servant or minister would have approved its tone. It is deliberately slanted to give Wells a far bigger part in the matter than he in fact played. Indeed, it was typical of his arrogance to try it on. He would have expected it to be considerably watered down by Nicholas. He must have been cock-a-hoop when he was unexpectedly told he could go ahead with it in its present form.'

'I can well see that he must have been in a state of spectacular fury when he discovered the truth,' said Milton. 'He's going to have a lot of explaining to do. I'm very grateful to you for letting me know about this.'

'I should be grateful if you could find some way of concealing from him the precise source of your information, Superintendent. It will make for bad relations. Many people would think I should have left you to find out for yourself. I don't intend to mention to my colleagues that it was I who told you.'

'When will it be common knowledge, sir?'

'In the department? I should think by mid-morning tomorrow.'

'In that case, sir, I shan't get in touch with Mr Wells until then. If he asks, I'll tell him I got an anonymous tip-off.'

'That is very considerate of you, Superintendent.'

'One must always try to protect one's informants, sir. I don't want you to think twice the next time you contemplate helping us.'

Sanders suddenly recollected Amiss's presence. 'I'm sorry, Robert. I forgot to invite you to give the Superintendent your views.'

'Don't worry, Douglas. I had nothing to add. As you know, I agree with your interpretation of events. I'm quite certain that Sir Nicholas hated Wells enough to have seized on this opportunity to discredit him. Nor do I think he would have let loyalty to his department hold him back. Lately, he didn't seem to have any respect at all for his colleagues.'

'I must say, Superintendent,' said Sanders reflectively, 'that though I am of course anxious that the murderer be found soon,

I am even more anxious to discover why Nicholas went off the rails as he seems to have done?'

'I can think of two reasons, connected with his private life, but I am at a complete loss to understand why he should take his private miseries out on two public figures. I hope to understand this before I finish the investigation.'

They said friendly goodbyes, and Amiss ushered Milton out. 'I hadn't imagined that you could stay quiet for so long,' said Milton, grinning at him.

'Long practice,' Amiss replied, grinning back. 'I've done well in the service by learning when to keep my mouth shut. Humility is a quality in short supply among graduate entrants. I decided long ago to give at least an appearance of it. It's made me very popular with my superiors.'

'See you later.'

'I can't wait. I'll see if I can't find some more motives, meanwhile.'

'Just you dare,' Milton grunted, as he stumped off back to the Yard.

Chapter Twenty-eight

Milton got through his discussions with his sergeants in half an hour. Then he spent several minutes sitting alone, staring at the grimy wall in front of him, going over the events of the past few days, the card-sorter in his head set for 'nagging doubts'. There was one that had been bothering him on and off since the previous morning. Who had sent the postcard to the Yard pointing the finger at Lady Clark and Martin Jenkins? Of course, as he had earlier imagined, it could be simply the work of a busybody, or of someone completely unconnected with the case who thought it was a lead the police should follow up. Alternatively, it could be the work of the murderer, seeking to distract attention from himself. That would mean it was either Nixon, Wells, Parkinson, Stafford or Shaw. It could hardly be Lady Clark's beloved son.

He called Romford in again.

'What's the news about the postcard?'

'The handwriting lads haven't come up with anything yet, sir. Block capitals, cheap ball-pen. Difficult.'

I know, Romford, I know. 'Have they had all the examples of handwriting we asked the suspects to provide?'

'They should have had them all by now, sir.'

Milton didn't really have much hope that anything would come of this. Still, he was impatient to have the possibility ruled out. A thought struck him.

'Have you held back a photocopy of the message?'

'Of course, sir,' said Romford in a wounded tone. He was very sensitive to any suggestion that he wasn't on the ball.

'Well done,' said Milton soothingly. 'Can you let me have it, please?'

He jammed it into his case and went off to the Star of India. As he had expected, Amiss was again there ahead of him.

Milton fell into his chair. 'What a day! Tell you what, let's go and eat at a brightly-lit table in one of those smart English places where the nobs go, and discuss all this in loud voices over Dover sole and saddle of lamb!'

'Lamb cutlets and chips on the menu here. Look—"with minty sauce." Guts not holding up too well, then? Mine are fine.'

'You're enjoying all this too much, Robert,' said Milton reprovingly. 'You must be in the wrong job. Why don't you join the force?'

'Christ, no. It's one thing playing at the wonder-boy assistant, but I don't fancy doing it professionally. I'm the weedy intellectual type. I never fancied doing anything dangerous.'

'Maybe you're right. Nobody's hit me in recent years, but I still have a couple of scars from Grosvenor Square in 1969.'

'Maybe you got them from me, Jim. I was an idealist in those days. In fact, one of the things that put me off demonstrations was the sight of what went on there. I got stuck in the middle of a real barney between a couple of tough coppers and a handful of hairy protesters, and I didn't enjoy it one single bit.'

'I put you down as the middle-of-the-road type—left-wing Tory if anything. I'll try those lamb chops.'

Amiss did the honours with the waiter, whose white jacket, Milton's trained eye noted, had borne the same pattern of stains for three evenings now.

'Right-wing Labour is more the mark. I've moved to the right since I joined the service and discovered pragmatism.'

'You mean you were well left-of-centre when you were recruited? I thought they only took moderates?'

'As long as you don't let your political views influence your judgement you can be anything short of a member of a party committed to the overthrow of the established order. The service assumes quite rightly that experience of the realities of government will dampen anyone's political ardour. I'd imagine you get proportionately more floating voters in the service than among the population as a whole. We tend to vote for a front bench rather than for a party.'

'You're too complicated a species for a simple policeman,' grumbled Milton. 'What about Sanders, then? He certainly came across with the goods. I thought you said they were all too cautious for that.'

'Sanders is rather different—I hadn't realized how different until I began to work for him. I think he's been inhibited by Sir Nicholas so far. He seems to be prepared to take risks now that he's got no one leaning on him. Not that he's going to change character entirely—he's been a civil servant too long for that, but he'll certainly loosen the reins on the department slightly. There are some senior people who believe in being a bit more open about what goes on in government. It's just that their style is cramped by the anal retentives of the old school. Anyway, what did you make of what Sanders told you?'

'What I said. I can't decide if it's a welcome or unwelcome piece of news. There seem to be more motives than opportunities in this case. Let me tell you about what came up today.'

'Bloody hell,' said Amiss, when Milton had finished his saga and his dreadful meal and was solacing himself with a brandy. 'What was Sir Nicholas trying to do on Monday morning? Start a riot?'

'Your guess is as good as mine. He certainly had the bit between his teeth. I don't think I'll ever understand what he was up to. It's bad enough trying to work out what everyone else was doing. Nixon had a motive; Wells at least two. Parkinson had one. So had Nigel. Lady Clark's statement that Sir Nicholas had been unpleasant to Stafford strengthens his. At least Jenkins and Shaw seem to be in the clear.'

'You haven't seen Shaw yet, have you?'

'No,' groaned Milton. 'He's getting cross about always being postponed in favour of the next hot suspect. I hope nothing crops up to stop me seeing him tomorrow.'

'Who else are you seeing?'

'Well, Stafford and Wells, of course. And I suppose I'd better go back and quiz Lady Clark about Nigel. If no one else looks particularly promising, I'll have to try out the theory that he killed his father in a rage and she helped him kill Gladys. I'll feel pretty silly suggesting it.'

'You haven't quite ruled out Jenkins, have you?'

'I have, really. As he said, it would have been pointless for him to kill Sir Nicholas, since he was going to get his wife anyway. IGGY isn't such an attractive committee that he'd kill to stay on it, is it?'

'God, no. It's incredibly tedious. Mind you, a lot of people do like to boast about being members of it; it makes them feel as if they're at the centre of things. But it would take a really dedicated Establishment climber to make that a reason for murder.'

'What's more, anybody with such a reason would presumably wait for a better opportunity to do the job. Whoever murdered Sir Nicholas took an enormous risk. It certainly can't have been premeditated.'

'You don't think Jenkins was lying about failing to find him, do you? Maybe he did and Sir Nicholas said something really foul about his wife. Welshmen are supposed to be hot-tempered, aren't they?'

'I suppose it's possible, Robert, but it really looks to me as if he wouldn't be the type to rise to that kind of provocation. He was going to get her away from Sir Nicholas. Wouldn't that have made him magnanimous?'

'I suppose it would,' sighed Amiss. 'I have to admit to an unworthy motive in trying to make a case against him. It would be very nice for the department if the whole thing proved to have nothing to do with us. The press will have the time of their lives if it emerges that it was either Nixon, Wells or Parkinson. Even Stafford wouldn't be too good from our point of view. It would cast doubt on our methods of arriving at decisions about grants.'

'Who's being an anal retentive now?'

'I'm not, am I? Be careful. I get upset when anyone suggests I'm turning into a civil-service stereotype. That's probably because it's true. One of my staff called me "a toffee-nosed fartarse" today.'

'I thought you were guaranteed respect from your subordinates?'

'You haven't met Phil. You'd better not, either. He doesn't think much of the pigs.'

'He seems to be an unexpected kind of person to recruit into your sober outfit.'

'You'd be surprised. Personnel are so desperate to get bright youngsters into the service that they'll accept all sorts of eccentricities now. There's a fellow downstairs who wears a nappy pin through his left ear. And Phil's favourite tee-shirt has "*bullshit*" printed across it. He wasn't allowed to wear it when Sir Nicholas was in the office, but hardly anyone else seems to mind. Sanders even likes it. He's appointed Phil his court jester. This afternoon, I was in with him, and Phil had been brought into the room to unpack some of Sanders's belongings. Sanders was in full flow about some esoteric aspect of policy. You'll have noticed that he's not above the occasional bureaucratic cliché. "You perceive my thrust?" he said at one point, and Phil turned round from where he was kneeling by a carton on the floor, stared him in the groin, and said "Snuffink to brag about". I thought for a moment Sanders was going to choke, and then he burst out laughing. Said he was pleased to have someone who recognized the absurdities of civil-service phraseology when he heard them. I wasn't too pleased at that reaction, I can tell you. It'll make the little sod impossibly cocky—not that he isn't that already.'

'You've cheered me up, Robert. I must be off. I've got some hard thinking to do tonight, and it's late already. Would you mind if I brought my wife along tomorrow night? I haven't had an evening with her all week, and she'd be interested in talking about the case. She's a psychologist, so she might have some insights into Sir Nicholas.'

Amiss agreed enthusiastically.

'One more thing before I go, and a very long shot.' He handed Amiss the photocopy Romford had provided. 'You don't know anybody who makes his capitals like that, do you? We're pretty sure they're disguised.'

'No, sorry. They could be anybody's. On a postcard, you said?'

'Yes.' Milton rose to go. 'A crank, probably, who thought he had a sense of humour.'

'But it isn't a joke. It's true about Jenkins and Lady Clark.'

'Oh, certainly. The postcard, though—it was one of those incredibly unfunny seaside things. Somebody's wife with a coalman.'

'Coalman?'

'Yes.'

'Sit down. I know who sent it.'

Chapter Twenty-nine

By midnight Milton had said good-night to Ann and had settled himself in his armchair to think things through again. The conversation with Amiss over the extra cup of coffee had taken on a more urgent tone than any previously. On Monday and Tuesday evenings, they'd pretty well made presentations to each other of evidence and hypotheses that they'd had time to digest individually. When Amiss dropped his bombshell about the postcard, they found themselves engaged in the kind of question-and-answer, thrust-and-parry dialogue that each was accustomed to having internally in striving for judgements and conclusions.

The postcard was from Sir Nicholas. Oh, God. How could it be? Come back to that later ... All right: what evidence? Amiss had seen it, blank, in old Nick's briefcase the week before—retrieving a draft so that Julia could correct a typing error. Sir Nicholas? A dirty postcard? He used to call Jenkins 'The Coalman'—Welsh prole, see? Amiss had been surprised by the postcard but had thought no more of it at the time: certainly hadn't connected it with Lady C. But the postmark? Eight hours after his death? Well, he'd hardly put it in his own out-tray, would he? And non-urgent mail from general offices—big mail-shots, for instance—was often collected in bulk by Post Office vans at close of play. Could easily sit around at the sorting-office and be franked mid-evening. Nothing to stop Sir Nicholas finding such a pile of mail in a nearby office and slipping the postcard into it. Possible enough, but what was he up to? That question again. The answer has to come from a broader pattern. General category of shit-stirring, for the moment. Why send it to the Police Commissioner? Highly moral man, Sir Peter; a long interview in one of the Sunday heavies just last week—importance of family life and so on. Besides, if Sir Nicholas was embarking, as seemed to be the case, on the most thorough-going campaign of mischief-making since … since … (Since Dennis the Menace? Hardly fitting …) he'd probably written to the Queen and the Archbishop of Canterbury as well. But what would the Commissioner have done about it in normal circumstances? Nothing. Wouldn't have been any of his business. Was Sir Nicholas *expecting* to be murdered, then? Planting clues for a posthumous revenge in case one of his victims *did* go berserk? Worth thinking about.

Pouring himself a drink, Milton could not clearly remember who had contributed what to the deductive process. Once again, he would have to take credit the next morning for inspired lateral thinking. If nudged, the handwriting experts could probably find enough resemblance—that manuscript speech in Sir Nicholas's study at home had plenty of capitals in it. Romford could be sent to get it. Having it proved that Sir Nicholas had sent the card would constitute a Pyrrhic victory, though. He might get a slap on the back from the A.C., but the trail to the murderer would have been blurred yet again. It would have been clearer had the postcard turned out to be a prurient hoax. Confusion worse confounded. Why couldn't he just once have a new piece of evidence which simplified things rather than fouling them up further?

He told himself harshly to drop the self-pity and start doing something constructive. He needed a clear head when he had his progress meeting the next morning. He put the bottle away, picked up a sheet of paper and began to write steadily.

Nigel Clark

Sir Nicholas Clark's murder

Motive: Sir Nicholas called him a pervert.
Opportunity: Plenty.

Pro:	Intensely emotional state matches risky and unpremeditated murder.
Con:	Nothing concrete. Claimed to be sorry for his father.
Action:	Temperament: fits of bad temper? Question friends.

Gladys Bradley's murder

Motive:	He could have known she overheard row with father.
Opportunity:	Excellent, if his mother helped him.
Pro:	Sudden recognition of Gladys on Tuesday—panic—paper knife.
Con:	His mother—moderating influence/common sense. Parricide under extreme provocation—light sentence. Murder of Gladys—throw the book at him.
Action:	As above. And try bullying Lady Clark

Martin Jenkins and Lady Clark

Sir N. (Jenkins)

Motive:	Lost his temper when Sir Nicholas insulted Lady Clark—putative.
Opportunity:	Good. Lost to view for at least five minutes.
Pro:	Very little.
Con:	Nothing to gain and much to lose.
Action:	Hot temper? As for Nigel Clark.

Gladys (Lady Clark)

Motive:	Gladys heard row. Jenkins saw Gladys and told Lady C.—putative.
Opportunity:	Excellent, bar Nigel's presence.
Pro:	Not much.
Con:	How could Jenkins have recognized Gladys? Would he really ask his beloved to murder for him?
Action:	As above. And probe Jenkins-Lady C.-Nigel relationship.

Harvey Nixon

Sir N.

Motive:	Blind rage.
Opportunity:	Several minutes unaccounted for.
Pro:	Cumulative provocation. A sneering remark—the last straw—from Sir N. all too likely.
Con:	Gained nothing. Why not get Sir N. sacked in revenge?
Action:	Trace earlier instances of Sir N's torments—any sign of consequential rage?

Gladys

Motive:	She'd certainly have recognized him, and he her. *N.B.* Of all the rows she might have heard, this the likeliest for reporting to her husband.
Opportunity:	Good. His office was next door and most people out to lunch.
Pro:	Obvious.
Con:	This suggests premeditation. How could he know she hadn't already talked? Of course, she was stupid enough to tell him, but if he'd *planned* such an interview, wouldn't he have planned the method as well? Do senior Cabinet Ministers notice clerical assistants' paper-knives?
Action:	Find out if he was in the habit of hanging round socialising in Sir N's outer office. 'Look at what Robert brought me back from Morocco, Secretary of State…'

Richard Parkinson

Sir N.

Motive:	Sir N. had ruined his career.
Opportunity:	As good as most other suspects.
Pro:	Revenge plus improved career prospects.
Con:	Why such a risky occasion? Many better opportunities.

| Action: | Check for evidence of improved career prospects in a post-Sir Nicholas world. Also for any extra provocation Monday morning. |

Gladys

Motive:	Similar to Nixon's.
Opportunity:	Reasonable. Least eminent eye-catching suspect so far—better chance of coming and going unnoticed.
Pro:	Obvious.
Con:	Same weapon problem as with Nixon. Entry/exit risky. No evidence of row with Sir N.
Action:	As above. And check as for Nixon re: socializing in outer office.

Milton stopped and sighed, lit a fat cigar whose opulence would have raised eyebrows at the Yard, and ploughed on. A weak brandy and soda after the next, perhaps.

Archibald Stafford

Sir N.

Motive:	Lost job because of Sir N's meddling. Lady Clark heard Sir N. insulting him on telephone. Was there a post-IGGY row—perhaps started by Stafford this time?
Opportunity:	Hadn't they all?
Pro:	Concealed the fact that Sir N. had insulted him.
Con:	Stood to gain nothing; and no sign that he *knew* Sir N. had fixed his waggon.
Action:	Get more from Lady Clark on that phone-call, then confront Stafford with it.

Gladys

Motive:	The usual.
Opportunity:	Minuscule. Outsider, so entry/exit require logged pass.
Pro:	Nothing.
Con:	She might have known him, but how would he know her? Risks of access. Weapon problem again.

| Action: | Send a bright plain-clothesman to try slipping through the building's security. |

Anticipating the A.C.'s reaction to this last measure, Milton grinned and mixed the nightcap stronger than he'd intended. Two to go.

Alfred Shaw

Sir N.

Motive:	Didn't like Sir N. calling him 'Sid'. Or maybe Sir N. had given him a duff tip on the St Leger.
Opportunity:	Yes. The only reason he's on the list.
Pro:	Nothing.
Con:	Everything.
Action:	Interview him. Perhaps some totally unsuspected motive.

Gladys

Motive:	The same and only reason anyone would do for Gladys: self-protection.
Opportunity:	Negligible. A public figure, never off T.V. In through the window, maybe, or in a false beard with a forged security pass.
Pro:	Nothing.
Con:	Everything.
Action:	As above.

Milton started a fresh sheet of paper for the last in the alphabet. He was glad that this one was his favourite suspect.

William Wells

Sir N.

Motive:	Made to look silly and lost his moment of glory at IGGY. Wife alerted to his affair. Sir N's lie about the £20 million would probably lose him his job and his seat in due course. Game, set and match.
Opportunity:	Yes.
Pro:	Known to have a bad temper.

| Con: | Fancies himself shrewd. Would have had to have lost control completely to risk his future for revenge. |
| Action: | Grill him again. He's been secretive. |

Gladys

Motive:	Certainly. And they knew each other by sight.
Opportunity:	Fine. Same corridor.
Pro:	Obvious. And he'd be good at self-justification. How could he serve his electorate from behind bars?
Con:	As many of the above, but no more.
Action:	Grilling.

Milton rested his pen for a moment and read through what he had written. He was about ready to rule out Shaw, Stafford, Jenkins and Lady Clark. The first two he had always thought very long shots for Gladys's murder, and even Stafford's slightly enhanced motive for murdering Sir Nicholas couldn't make up for the difficulty he would have in finding the unfortunate witness. Still, he would have to go through the motions of interviewing him again, as he would have to go through the motions with Shaw. He wasn't again going to be caught neglecting routine. He would initiate the security check the following morning, and, later, send C.I.D. constables around the building with photographs of Shaw and Stafford to check that no one had seen them on Tuesday. All the other actions would go ahead, including upsetting Lady Clark, though he was morally certain that she couldn't have connived at Gladys's murder. The cowardly stabbing of an innocent bystander to cover up an all too understandable hot-blooded murder? Indefensible, in every sense of the word. So Nigel was probably out too.

He was back to the three favourite suspects again—Nixon, Parkinson and Wells. At least he now had in Wells a front-runner. It should be possible to convince the Assistant Commissioner that Wells's motive was now so strong that there was hope of breaking him. Today's new evidence should at least win him another twenty-four hours on the case.

Thursday Morning

Chapter Thirty

'You don't sound very optimistic, darling. Shall I cancel the Paris tickets?'

'Put the pessimistic tone down to an overdraft on the sleep account. You know I need eight hours at least one night in three. No, hold the tickets till this evening. You never know, someone may present me with a pukka clue today. A bloodstained foot-print might do the trick.'

'You'd probably find all your suspects were wearing the same size official-issue shoes. I'll keep my fingers crossed for you anyway. See you in the Star of India tonight. I'm looking forward to meeting your mole. How will I recognize him if you're not there?'

'He'll be cowering in the darkest corner swigging gin, brief-case under chair.'

Milton stuffed his scribblings of the early morning into an inside pocket and followed Ann out of the front door. The sunshine made him feel unreasonably buoyant. He was sud-denly ready to take them all on. The murderer must be feeling extremely twitchy; the right sort of pressure applied at the right time and with the right force might break him down. Surely Milton had enough on Wells to reduce him to a gibbering wreck. He would find that a pleasure even on a less salubrious day. Yes, definitely the weather for illuminating the dark corners of the killer's soul.

His first nasty shock of the day was the news that the morning meeting would be held in the Commissioner's office. He tried to look nonchalant about this when Romford told him, but as he delivered his orders for the day half his mind was grappling with the implications of this upgrading of the investigation. It had unpleasant connotations of worry on-high.

The Commissioner was wearing that grave look which was so appropriate when he made public statements about the rising crime rate. He waved his minions to their chairs and began unpromisingly:

'The Home Secretary tells me that the Prime Minister is gravely worried that this murder is still unsolved.'

Milton opened his mouth to protest that he'd only had two and half days on it. He caught a warning look on the Assistant Commissioner's face and shut it again.

'I have told him that I am entirely satisfied that this investigation has been given its due priority, and that I do not propose to neglect the other urgent work of the police force simply because a couple of politicians have found themselves mixed up in a murder case.'

Milton's relief must have shown. The Commissioner directed a glare at him. 'And now, Superintendent, I should be grateful for some indication that I was correct in taking up this attitude. Would you please explain to me exactly how far you have got, and what steps you propose to take to bring this case to a speedy conclusion?'

Thanks for nothing, thought Milton. How the hell was he supposed to get on with his work if he was always having to justify himself to his superiors? Still, he supposed he should be grateful to the old man for standing up for his subordinates. He could have given in meekly and promised to send in some bigger guns. Milton had no doubt that this was precisely what he would do if he wasn't satisfied by the report he got now. He blessed his industry of the night before and got out his notes.

As he went through his analysis, he was pleased to note that the Commissioner was growing aghast, as the Assistant

Commissioner grew smug. That could only mean that Milton was reinforcing the accounts the A.C. had been giving of the complexity of the case and the energy going into it. He permitted himself a few flourishes and dramatic pauses towards the end.

'Heavens above, Sir Nicholas must have been out of his mind!' The Commissioner's foulest blasphemy. 'What was he trying to do? Provoke the whole lot of them to murder him?'

Wait until he hears later today about the postcard, thought Milton to himself. *If he thinks it's a rich brew now ...*

They talked around it for several minutes. The general conclusion was the one Milton had already reached; either Sir Nicholas had reached such a point of rage and despair that he was trying to hurt everyone, or, even more incredible, he was actually trying to incite one or more people to attack him. The brass favoured the more conservative view, and Milton went along with them. Until the handwriting boys had followed up his superhuman hunch, he would have to.

'There's no doubt about its being murder, I suppose,' said the Commissioner. 'He couldn't have found some ingenious way of dropping the sculpture on his own head?'

'No, sir. And besides, that wouldn't explain the murder of Mrs Bradley.'

'That could have been an unconnected event,' said the A.C..

'We have, of course, not ignored such a possibility, sir, but her husband is in the clear and we can't find any reason for anyone else who knew her well to have wanted to kill her. She had no money and apparently no involvements outside her home and office. I really think we must suppose, at least for the moment, that she became a target when she chanced upon an altercation after the Monday morning meeting.'

'We know he had a row with his son. Isn't it reasonable to suppose that that was what she heard? And aren't you wrong therefore to make him a class-two suspect?'

'Not when there is ample evidence that Jenkins, Stafford, Nixon and Wells also had reason and opportunity for a showdown.'

'All right, Jim,' said the Commissioner. *Christian name again.* His sigh of relief went unnoticed. He was going to be let get on with this on his own. 'I really can't find much to criticize about your handling of the case, although I'm a little perturbed about the delay in finding out where Nigel Clark worked.' Milton blessed his own adroitness over the private detective's receipt. The case records were ambiguous about when it was found. 'Still, one can't avoid occasional lapses, and your skill in handling the suspects is undeniable. Carry on as you suggest. I'll hold off the politicians for another few days.'

Milton felt a warm glow as he left the room. Maybe he'd get a promotion out of this yet. He hoped it would be at the expense of William Wells. He didn't enjoy sending people he liked off to prison.

'You've got fifteen minutes before Stafford arrives, sir,' said Romford. 'There's been an urgent call for you from someone who refuses to give his name. Said he'd ring back about now.'

Amiss again? Milton just had time to instruct that someone be despatched to Kensington for Sir Nicholas's manuscript before the phone rang.

A secretary established the caller's identity as the editor of a Sunday newspaper—one of those specializing in victimization in the name of public morality. Leaving the worthwhile scandals of corruption or misuse of power to its less prosperous competitors, it preferred to ruin the lives of those guilty only of sexual indiscretion. Milton bit back on his disgust and began the conversation on a polite note.

It got harder to maintain as the nasty, evil-minded little hypocrite's story unfolded. The voice purred on about the public's right to know, concern for our national security, sympathy for the fine job the police force was doing in upholding law and order, anxiety to see justice done—the clichés piling up in proportion to the stature of the unfortunate, who was in for the old mud-slinging treatment. The figure in the pillory was Harvey Nixon.

The bare essentials were straightforward enough. One of the *Enquirer*'s staff, Susan Taylor, had received a hand-printed note suggesting that she might fruitfully occupy herself by finding out where Nixon usually went on Sunday evenings. Miss Taylor was a hard-working and ambitious reporter, the editor claimed, committing herself to ensuring that our leaders conducted themselves at all times with the integrity which the public rightly expected. This Milton translated to himself: The unscrupulous bitch wanted to rise in her profession by sniffing out signs of sexual unorthodoxy among senior politicians in a shaky government.

So dedicated was she, her editor smarmed on, that she gave up her Sunday nights for several weeks in following Nixon to an address which proved to be that of a well set-up call-girl. Further research indicated that other regular clients included two judges, three M.P.s and a handful of senior civil servants. The lady specialized in Establishment figures.

'None of them was acting illegally,' said Milton.

'Ah, but she also went in for Embassy clients, not all of them from friendly countries.'

Milton looked at his telephone incredulously. He wasn't going to be landed with a re-run of the Keeler affair, was he?

'Mr Nixon isn't by any stretch of the imagination a defence risk, sir.'

'That would be for the government to decide when the story broke.'

'You mean that you were going to print this story and ruin Nixon without any solid reason to suppose he was doing anything worse than visiting a call-girl? He's a divorced man, dammit, with virtually no time to himself.'

'There's no need to take that tone, Superintendent. I have been weighing up the case for and against.'

And I know which way you'd like to come down, you nasty little shit, thought Milton. He was feeling sick.

'Why didn't you inform me of this before?' he asked aggressively. 'You must have known it might be relevant to our enquiries.'

'I didn't know about it until last night, when Miss Taylor returned from a much-needed holiday. I believe in giving my reporters a lot of freedom to follow up promising leads without always running to me for approval.'

'I want to see that tip-off note immediately.'

'I'm sorry, Superintendent, Miss Taylor didn't think it was worth preserving. She destroyed it weeks ago. All she can say about it is that it had a Westminster postmark.'

Chapter Thirty-one

With a perfunctory expression of gratitude, Milton slammed the phone down. Romford came in to say that Stafford had arrived, and was told to hold him for a couple of minutes. *Think it through.* The odds were that the anonymous note showed the fine Italian hand of Sir Nicholas again, though he'd probably never be able to prove it. Assuming it did, how could he have known about the Sunday-evening peccadilloes? Unless Nixon had been dreadfully incautious, there were two obvious ways: either there had been some trailing done or one of the other clients had gossiped. Which, in turn, meant the prostitute talked to client A about client B. Unlikely; these girls knew the value of discretion.

He summoned Romford and told him to have the call-girl interrogated—no time to do it himself. All he wanted were dates and times of Nixon's visits and the names of her other clients. He looked at his watch. Ten-fifteen. Word about Wells and the newspaper article should be around the department by now. Romford was instructed to make appointments with Wells, Nixon and Lady Clark—preferably in that order. He reminded Milton that he would not be free until he had seen both Stafford and Shaw, who had indicated that his patience was running out. Milton hesitated. He couldn't face putting Shaw off again, but it would be absurd to waste his time today on such an unlikely prospect. He had been getting obsessional about seeing all the suspects himself. One of his inspectors or sergeants could stand in for him.

'But whoever does it is to get a complete statement of how often they met and exactly what Shaw thought of him,' he warned. Romford went off, speculating on what was making Milton state the obvious all the time in giving instructions.

He seemed to have taken that lapse over Nigel Clark too much to heart. It was a good thing that he, Romford, wasn't the type to get upset. Someone had to keep his head. Though mind you, he couldn't blame the Super for getting cross about this new development. He reflected primly that these top-shelf types didn't half go in for irregular sex. One adulterer, one adulteress, one homosexual, one bachelor knocking off a married woman and now a divorced man visiting a call-girl. Romford reflected on his model family life and began to compose the sermon on the sins of the flesh he would give the next time his chapel called on him. By the time he lifted the telephone, his mind had strayed to a fantasy of what the call-girl probably looked like.

Milton was short with Stafford. He told him sharply that he had reason to believe he had given a distorted account of the phone-call he had had with Sir Nicholas. The industrialist looked suitably abashed.

'I'm sorry, Superintendent. I admit I held back some of it, but I couldn't see how that would do any harm. Since I knew I didn't kill him, I couldn't see why I needed to confuse the issue by strengthening my motive.'

'It does great harm, Mr Stafford, when people implicated in a murder enquiry take it upon themselves to decide what is and is not relevant. Don't you realize that I need all the evidence I can get about the behaviour of Sir Nicholas before he was murdered?'

Stafford abandoned his misunderstood look. 'You're right, of course, Superintendent. I was looking at it from my own point of view, not yours. I'll tell you everything this time.'

He went on with what was by now a drearily familiar tale of outrageous goading. Sir Nicholas had been so unfriendly and unsympathetic on the telephone that Stafford had eventually accused him of setting the department and the grants board against him.

'He said he had indeed, and was proud of it. I was past it and should come to terms with the fact. He said if I liked, I could talk to him about it after the Monday morning meeting.'

'What did you say?'

'I said "go to hell" and put the phone down.'

'You didn't speak to him after the meeting?'

'No, Superintendent. I didn't ever want to speak to him again. I was afraid I might lose my temper. He came up to me just before the meeting started, but I turned away and began to talk to someone else.'

Milton believed him. Stafford had been clutching at his last shreds of dignity. He couldn't imagine him wanting to get involved in a shouting match which might attract witnesses. He let him go.

Romford came in looking pleased with himself. 'Lady Clark will see you in half an hour, sir, and Mr Wells will be free between twelve thirty and one fifteen. Mr Nixon says he could see you after that, but he's got to answer questions in the House at two forty-five and would prefer to see you later if you don't mind. Prime Minister's Question Time starts at three fifteen and he'll slip away as soon as he can. He suggests you go to his room in the Commons about half three and he'll be along as quickly as possible.'

'Three thirty will be fine, tell him.'

Milton set off for Kensington and Lady Clark. He was pre-occupied with this new story about Harvey Nixon. It might be totally irrelevant, but he feared it wasn't. If Sir Nicholas knew about Nixon's sexual activities, he surely wouldn't have missed the chance to tell him, before or on Monday. He had been planning an Armageddon and Milton couldn't imagine him wasting good material like the news that a smut-sheet was on Nixon's trail. Could even the gentlest man have kept his head when he heard that? If it hadn't been for Gladys, Milton might well have asked to be relieved of the case on personal grounds. Sir Nicholas deserved to be in the dock, not whoever had been driven to murder him. His killer deserved a decoration. But not Gladys's. He resolved to think regularly about her from now on.

There was something about the world he was moving in on this investigation that blunted his zeal. Gladys was more real to him, although he'd only seen her dead.

He got to South Kensington quicker than he had expected and killed a few minutes gaping absently into shop windows. His eye caught a display of pale furniture, rich carpets and expensive knick-knacks. Leaning casually against the reproduction Adam fireplace, its face set in a refined smile, was a mannequin dressed with restraint, elegance and classic good taste. It bore a marked resemblance to Lady Clark. Madame Tussaud's could put it straight into the Chamber of Horrors if she turned out to have murdered Gladys, though he supposed they wouldn't think it a gory enough killing to warrant her inclusion. Still, you could never tell what would seize the public imagination. Despite all the popular contempt for Whitehall, there was a national appetite for shenanigans among its high-ups. Milton thought about Nixon again and groaned inwardly. At least he was having the decency not to interrogate him before he had to perform in the House. He glanced at his watch again and walked briskly towards Lady Clark's house.

'You've come to rebuke me for not telling you about Nigel, haven't you, Superintendent?' she said, as they sat down.

'Among other things, Lady Clark.'

'Look,' she said, and there were tears in her eyes, 'I told you about my marriage and my adultery. Could you seriously expect me to tell you also that my only child had turned out homosexual? It wasn't relevant. I knew he had had an argument with Nicholas about Ronald, but he couldn't have killed him.'

'You can't be sure of that.'

'I can. Not just because I know it to be totally out of character for Nigel to raise a hand against anyone, but because whatever Nicholas said to him about Ronald, he couldn't really hurt him deeply. Nigel is in love, just as I am. In a similar position, I would have been able to take anything Nicholas said against Martin because he couldn't hurt me any more. He had lost that power long before his death.'

'But Nigel was very upset by what his father said.'

'There's a difference between being upset and being wounded deeply enough to want to strike, Superintendent. I assure you, I have never seen Nigel so happy. It's because he's developed so much emotionally since he met Ronald that I've been able to accept their relationship.'

'You can't expect me to see it quite so simply, Lady Clark.'

'No, of course I can't. But you must accept that he has an alibi for Mrs Bradley's murder.'

'I know he has been given an alibi by his mother, as I know his mother has been given an alibi by him.'

'I suppose I should feel insulted by the implications of that remark, but I can't. I've been expecting it. You think Nigel might have lied to protect me as I might have lied to protect him, and I'm in no position to prove that that didn't happen. I can only say that while I have a great deal of sympathy with whoever murdered Nicholas, I feel a violent contempt for whoever killed that poor woman to keep himself out of jail. You can believe that or not as you wish.'

'Did Nigel know about you and Mr Jenkins?'

'No. I didn't want to burden him with my troubles. He had enough of his own.'

'Have they ever met?'

'Never.'

Milton had already decided to believe one suspect this morning. He didn't know if he could afford to believe two. Maybe the whole damn lot of them were plausible liars and he was getting gullible. He contemplated going through with bullying Lady Clark in the way he had intended. He couldn't. It wouldn't sound convincing. In his heart he believed she was about as capable of having anything to do with Gladys's death as Ann was.

'All right, Lady Clark. We'll let it go at that for the moment. Can I ask you something else? Did Sir Nicholas ever go out alone on Sunday nights?'

The question took her aback.

'Sunday nights, Superintendent? Not often. There was a period a few months ago when he went out an awful lot at weekends and stayed out very late many evenings during the week. I suppose he went out on a few Sundays. I couldn't be precise about it unless I looked at my diary and thought about it for a while.'

'Where did he go?'

'I don't know. He used just to say he wanted to walk and think for a while. Sometimes he said he was working at the office. I wondered for a while if he had found somebody too, but when he went back to his normal habits after a few weeks I decided he had probably just been overworking. What do you think he was doing?'

'I don't know, Lady Clark,' lied Milton. 'I haven't got enough to go on. I was just following up a possible lead.'

He knew all right, he thought, as he walked back to the tube. He would lay heavy odds that Sir Nicholas had spent his spare time—as Susan Taylor was to do later—following Harvey Nixon.

Chapter Thirty-two

Amiss had started his day in a state of vindictive contentment. He was pleased with the thought that William Wells was going to have hell to pay. He hoped Milton would give him a real going-over. With luck he'd turn out to be the murderer. So what if some of the ripples did spread to the department? From what Milton had told him of the other suspects, they all seemed like reasonably decent people. If anyone was guilty it should be the greatest available shit.

He had the joy of being present when Nixon and Sanders told Wells what they thought of him. Sanders necessarily had to be rather circumspect; it was an embarrassment that his predecessor had been the one to set Wells off on his disastrous trail. Nixon didn't have any such inhibitions, however. Amiss had never seen him in a temper before and was surprised at how loud and offensive he could be. Not that he said a word that either of those witnessing the dressing-down would have disagreed with, unless Sanders, perhaps, found the expression 'prize cunt' a bit unparliamentary. Amiss doubted it though. He was pretty sure that his own smile of approval had been mirrored in Sanders's face.

It was worth staying in the civil service if he was going to have treats like this from time to time. He was certain Sanders had brought him into the meeting as a sort of thank-you for having put up with Sir Nicholas for so long. The only disappointment was that Wells didn't seem as upset as he might be. Although he had looked a bit shaken initially at the discovery that Nixon could turn nasty, he had lapsed into sullenness by the end. He just kept muttering about putting his constituents first, and he was visibly pleased that the Prime Minister had decided to reconsider the decision immediately. He was talking to colleagues on the phone now. Sanders—and indeed Nixon—had pleaded with the P.M. to stick to his guns, but the issue had never really been in doubt. It would take a brave man indeed to put his small majority to the test over something as potentially explosive as a public clash between two of its ministers.

'That was a right slaggin'-down ole Nixon gave Wells,' observed Phil with appreciation as Amiss went back into his office.

'What do you know about it?' asked Amiss incredulously. It was far too early for the news to have got round the department.

'I 'appened to be in the corridor, didn't I? I 'eard Nixon shoutin' at 'im about 'is bein' a traitorous little shit. Good for Nixon. Never thought 'e 'ad it in 'im.'

Amiss cuffed him moodily and retired to his desk. Something would have to be done about Phil. He seemed to regard the department as a vehicle for his entertainment. Still, maybe that was a healthy viewpoint. It was better to be entertained by your job than crushed by it. God knows he deserved a few chuckles himself after his time with Sir Nicholas, although it was arguable that the very traits in Sir Nicholas that made him hard to bear had been the direct cause of all the unusual entertainment he had got that week. The new boss, too, had come courtesy of the same chain of events. Not for the first time recently, he caught himself in internal debate in classic civil servicese—'on the one hand' balancing 'on the other', and all implications given due weight. And to think there was a time when he'd dreamt of being a rock-and-roll star.

He resisted the temptation to further introspection and began to read through the final brief for Harvey Nixon's Question Time that afternoon. He hoped Nixon would recover sufficiently by then to offer a good account of himself. There were enough stories flying round about his exhibition on Monday, and none of them was charitable. Amiss bet there would be an unusually good turn-out of M.P.s this afternoon. You could normally count on there being no more than a handful for any uncontroversial session to do with a department generally regarded as boring. But they would be there in force today to see the performance at the Despatch Box of a man whose career seemed as good as finished, and who might even be a murderer. The newspapers hadn't been able to give the list of suspects, of course, but those in the know had a pretty fair idea of who had been ruled out, and who were still receiving police attention.

The brief suggested that Nixon could expect some problems that afternoon with Question 1, which concerned the government's refusal to provide the money for a new glass-recycling plant in Wales. Amiss didn't agree. He couldn't see Nixon being attacked as hard on this one today as he might be at other times. The House of Commons was fundamentally a club—its members might privately enjoy each others' discomfiture, but they wouldn't publicly attack a man who was known to be in trouble. That would be bad form, and only the most inexperienced or nasty members would try it on. In any case, the figures that had won the case against the Welsh plant were incontrovertible, and, although Nixon could be a bit shaky on statistics, Parkinson would be there to brief him if he got into any difficulty. The next item, an apparently innocuous question about the chemical-recycling plant, was a different matter. Someone was sure to find an opportunity to raise the issue of Wells's article. Still, the P.M. had promised a revised or reinforced decision by lunchtime, and Nixon and Sanders could sort out then what was to be said about it.

Phil was clearly bored. He had decided to persecute Julia. He had raised his head from his book and was chanting 'Julia, light of my life, fire of my loins. My sin, my soul. Ju-li-a: the tip of the tongue taking a trip of three steps down the palate to tap, at three on the teeth. Ju. Lee. A.'

'He is adapting the opening lines from *Lolita*, Julia,' said Amiss patiently. 'Listen, you little sod, if you had the faintest idea how to pronounce the English language you would know that none of those syllables taps on the teeth. What are you doing reading, anyway? There must be plenty for you to do.'

'You're always sayin' that, and there never is. Bad management, I call it. You're not organizin' your staff properly.'

Amiss went over to look. As he had feared, Phil was absolutely right. All the mail had been logged or despatched. The filing had been done. Phil's desk was clear. He looked round for something to criticize.

'Have you checked that all Sir Nicholas's official appointments have been transferred into Sanders's diary? I only told him about the ones for this week.'

'I couldn't, could I? I told you it had disappeared.'

'You couldn't find Sir Nicholas's diary?'

'Nah. And don't tell me I never looked properly. I told you, I looked in Sanders's office and I've been through all the drawers and cabinets.'

'Oh, go back to *Lolita* then.'

'Wiv pleasure.'

Where the hell was that diary? It didn't matter that much. He should himself have a record of most of the important engagements in it. It was just that he hadn't transferred any made on the previous Friday. He was sure he had put it back on Gladys's desk when he had finished with Sanders. Maybe the police had taken it away. He must check with Milton, although he couldn't imagine that they would have done that without telling him.

The missing diary gnawed away at the back of his mind while he dealt with phone calls and the continual flow of pieces of paper. It was nearly midday before he began to think it might have some bearing on one or both of the murders. The entering down of Sir Nicholas's appointments was Gladys's prerogative. Indeed, it was a duty she carried out with great ceremony. She seemed to regard the diary as a kind of archive, and couldn't be dissuaded from noting appointments even retrospectively when they were of no importance. Amiss had often felt irritated when he saw her writing down the time at which some colleague had dropped in on Sir Nicholas, but it wasn't worth upsetting her about it. If she wanted to add to her burdens she might as well be left to it. Criticism only made her tearful.

What could have been in it that would make anyone steal it?—for suddenly that seemed the most likely explanation for its disappearance. It could only be a record of someone having called on Sir Nicholas—someone who had reason to want the information suppressed. The murderer, in other words. How would he know she had entered the information? Because she would probably have asked him his name. (Even if she knew the name she might well have asked him how to spell it.) He'd have had to steal it as well as kill her.

Amiss gave up all pretence of work. This had to be sorted out. It completely altered the official view on the reason for Gladys's murder. If the diary really had been stolen, it must record a meeting between Sir Nicholas and the murderer at some time when Gladys was alone in the office. Could that be as early as Friday evening? No. More probably Monday morning. He went over to Julia.

'I'm trying to get the staff rotas for the next few weeks worked out, Julia, and I'm not sure who's been coming in early and staying late over the past week.'

'Last week George was on early and Bernard was on late. This week Gladys was on early and I was on late. Not that she was early on Tuesday. I think she'd got confused. Phil's doing early now.'

The meeting must have been Monday morning, then. Gladys should in theory have been in at 8.15 to man the telephones until the others began to arrive from 9.00 onwards. Where did that get him? What was so significant about someone having been in to see Sir Nicholas early? Maybe there had been an argument? But that brought up the old problem of how the murderer could have known Gladys wouldn't say anything about it until much later. Was it the mere fact of the meeting? That would point to two possibilities: either one of the suspects had lied about not seeing Sir Nicholas before IGGY, or the murderer was someone not on the existing list—someone who was in Embankment Tower and had the opportunity to kill him after IGGY, but whose name meant nothing to the police. Amiss's heart bled for Milton at the very thought of the latter explanation. The first one seemed peculiar as well. Why should any of the suspects lie about having seen Sir Nicholas? It wouldn't have made the evidence against them any more incriminating; they all had good official reasons to visit him. Unless they lied first and then remembered later that they could be found out.

Amiss's head was spinning. Wait. The security staff would have a record of any outsiders who had entered the building on Monday morning. That would look after any early visitors to Sir Nicholas except those with passes—Nixon, Wells and Parkinson. There was even a chance that it would be remembered if they had passed through reception at an unusually early hour. He'd have to try to get a message through to Milton to start an urgent check on the usual suspects and a new range of possibles. In the meantime he would see if he could find out about the insiders.

Thursday Afternoon

Chapter Thirty-three

The worried girl who shared Wells's outer office gave Milton a message to ring Romford. The hot news was already stale as far as Milton was concerned, but he put up a good pretence of modest surprise that his hunch about Sir Nicholas and the anonymous postcard had paid off. He cut short Romford's rather plodding speculations about Sir Nicholas's motivation and asked to be brought up-to-date on anything else. 'Not much, sir. Inspector Gifford says that he couldn't find out anything from Alfred Shaw that links him with Sir Nicholas. He's off now interviewing that call-girl. Should be back about half-an-hour from now.'

Milton thought rapidly. 'Tell him to meet me in the pub across the road from the House of Commons. I'll get there between half one and two.'

'Right, sir. Oh, one other thing. Your wife rang up. She said it was urgent. You can get her at her office about one thirty.'

It must be Amiss again, thought Milton as he rang off. This was becoming ludicrous. He wasn't more than fifty yards away from Amiss's office. He didn't need to communicate with him by such a convoluted route. He muttered an excuse to the girl and went down to Amiss's room. It was empty apart from a youth in his late teens, sporting an earring and ragged jeans, bent intently over the *Financial Times*. Milton was momentarily surprised at the incongruity of it. Then he spotted the legend on the tee-shirt. Of course, the court jester.

'Is Mr Amiss available?' he enquired politely.

'Nah. 'E's buggered off to lunch. 'E'll be back about two but 'e's goin' out straight away. 'Oo shall I say wanted 'im?'

'It doesn't matter,' said Milton hastily. 'It was nothing of importance.' *So I'll bugger off out of it.*

He returned to Wells's office and put Amiss out of his mind. He'd have time to ring Ann before he saw Gifford in the pub. Going straight through to the modest inner sanctum, he found Wells looking a shade defiant.

'Yes, Superintendent? How can I help you?'

'By telling me with no more evasion or half-truths exactly what passed between you and Sir Nicholas between last Friday and his murder.'

'Come now, Superintendent. There's no need to put it like that. I answered all your questions frankly. I didn't see any reason to tell you things that didn't seem relevant.'

'I am sick and tired of being told what is relevant or irrelevant to my job. I want to know what happened between you over that misleading article you published yesterday, and I want to know why you concealed information which might be vital to police enquiries. Are you going to tell me everything now, or am I going to have to ask you to come over to the Yard for a more formal interrogation?'

'Well, of course I'll help you now, Superintendent. I can't possibly come over to the Yard. I've got to be in the House this afternoon.'

'You had better get one thing very clear, Mr Wells. You *will* come with me unless I am satisfied that you have told me all I want to know. If you think you can impress me by talking grandiosely about your duties as a junior minister or as an M.P. you are mistaken. You wouldn't be the first of them to have been taken into custody.'

Milton observed Wells's shocked silence with satisfaction. There was nothing like a low blow for bringing a bully to heel.

Wells began to talk. He was almost babbling. His story was circumstantially the same as Douglas Sanders's. The only differences were those of emphasis. Wells's account of his own behaviour was of a fighter for the just cause being blocked at every turn by the weak, the conservative or the naturally obstructive. He had, though, believed that his persuasiveness and the superiority of his argument would triumph. Harvey Nixon had told him that he wouldn't fight for the loan, but Wells had been sure that his own mates would carry the day in Cabinet. Sir Nicholas had dropped the odd remark to him suggesting that the decision was likely to go against the department, and had even congratulated Wells on the way in which he had run his campaign.

'But Sir Nicholas wasn't on your side, was he? You said you and he didn't get on well.'

'We weren't on the same side, but he was very friendly for a change over this whole business. Said he saw my point and was very impressed by my tactics. That was why I believed him when he said he would approve my article even though Nixon wouldn't like it.'

Milton gazed open-mouthed at Wells. Could even the most ambitious fool believe that a sane Permanent Secretary would urge a junior minister to boast publicly that he had won a battle against his own Secretary of State and his own department? Amiss had impressed on him how important loyalty was supposed to be.

'Surely that was an inconceivably disloyal thing for a civil servant to do to his minister?'

'Well, Sir Nicholas said that Nixon was such a lousy Secretary of State he had it coming.'

'And you seriously believed him?'

'Well, I suppose I wanted to,' said Wells with sudden honesty.

'Weren't you afraid of losing your job?'

'No. There's an election coming up reasonably soon and my main concern is to keep my seat. That article would have swung it.'

'You didn't worry about how Mr Nixon—or the Prime Minister for that matter—would have felt about it?'

'Why should I? They're both on their way out. I can afford to wait a couple of years for a ministerial job.'

Milton suddenly realized why Wells had told no one the article was coming out.

'You let that article appear yesterday without notifying your colleagues because you wanted to embarrass them?'

'That's right. They're having to reconsider the decision right now. If it goes my way, I win. If it goes against me, I win too, by resigning in protest at having been misled. I won't have any trouble about getting the local electors to see it as a bureaucrats' botch-up. If the civil service had known on Monday that the article was going to appear they'd have been able to pre-empt me.'

Of all the corrupt little weasels Milton had come across, this one took the biscuit. How was it possible for anyone to think like this and still make it in politics?

'I understand your recent actions now.' He was damned if he was going to call this Judas 'sir'. 'However, local information is that you tried on Monday afternoon to get the article withdrawn.'

'Yes. I did. I wasn't thinking clearly then. I admit I was in a bit of a panic. But when I discovered it was too late, I decided I had better turn the whole business to my advantage. That's what being a good politician is all about, you know.'

Milton wondered if Wells was showing his contempt in displaying himself as openly as this to someone who couldn't affect his career. He thought not. Wells probably thought he would be impressed. He hoped the next question would wipe the condescending expression off his face.

'Your panic must have been considerable when you heard the news on Monday morning. Your anger must have been even greater since it led you to kill Sir Nicholas.'

Wells's face was sagging, all right, but whether with surprise or fear Milton couldn't tell.

'You can't believe that. You haven't the faintest shred of evidence for it. Nixon had just as much reason to be furious with Sir Nicholas.'

'I'm not talking about Mr Nixon. I'm talking about you. You had a first-class motive. In fact you had three, which puts you well ahead of the field.'

It was fear now, Milton was pleased to observe.

'Look, Superintendent. You're getting this all wrong. Look at it from my point of view. Sir Nicholas had put me in an embarrassing position by having called in Nixon to take my place at the Industry and Government Group meeting. He had also upset my wife. Neither of those things were more than minor irritants. I admit that I was upset when I discovered he had misled me over the article, but killing him wouldn't have made any difference. He would have got into trouble over it too.'

'He could have denied seeing it.'

'I didn't think of that.'

I wonder how smart this bloke really is. Bluff, double-bluff, counter-bluff, subterfuge, self-deception. 'When did he tell you that he had misled you?'

'Just before the meeting began. I had just been turned out of my seat at the conference table to make way for Nixon when Sir Nicholas whispered to me.'

'What did he say?'

Wells looked unhappy. 'If I tell you the truth you'll probably think it helps the case against me.'

'If you don't tell me the truth I can assure you it will help the case against you far more. I should point out, too, that Sir Nicholas may have been overheard, and I intend to make a most thorough investigation of that possibility. Stop prevaricating and tell me now, exactly what he said.'

Wells was wriggling with embarrassment. 'He said "A letter has just gone to Chemical Recycling telling them that the Cabinet has rejected their application. Your nasty little career will be finished when your article appears."'

For the first time, Milton felt an upsurge of admiration—almost liking—for Sir Nicholas. The man who had done this to Wells couldn't be all bad.

'Did you speak to him again?'

'No, Superintendent. I admit I went looking for him after the meeting, but I couldn't see him in the lavatory or the corridor. I thought he must have left. I swear I didn't kill him.'

Milton gave up. He wasn't going to break Wells now. It would take more evidence or someone new to do that. As he passed through the outer office he made a call to Ann. 'Deep Throat was on again,' she said. 'He says it's important you try to see him in the House of Commons this afternoon. He'll be with the Secretary of State's briefing team.'

'Did he tell you what it was about?'

'No, he was going to, but I think someone came into the room. He couldn't have had any other reason for saying "Sorry I can't talk any more, darling, but I've got to rush."'

Chapter Thirty-four

Inspector Gifford was in St Stephen's Tavern when Milton arrived. He was sipping a half-pint and gazing lasciviously at a group of Scandinavian girls who were occupying half the small bar. Their lissom attractions did nothing for Milton. They all looked hyper-fit, bred for the tennis court and the après-ski disco. Perversely, he let his waistline sag as he passed them. The other half of the bar was dominated by a group of office workers out on a celebration. Their laughter had the hysterical edge that characterized ill-assorted groups bound together by bondage to a common employer. They were cementing their alliance with out-of-practice bonhomie fuelled by hasty rounds of drinks purchased from a kitty.

'Let's leave, Jack. We can't talk here. We'll take a walk instead.'

Gifford downed his beer and followed Milton into the street. They walked down to the Embankment and turned east to stroll slowly along by the river.

'Sorry to have dragged you away from your tube murder, Jack, but I've been up to my ears.'

'I've enjoyed it, sir. It makes a nice change, a bit of sex.'

'Well, I'm glad our call-girl was rewarding, but can we get Alf Shaw out of the way before you tell me about her?'

Gifford began to laugh and Milton looked at him in bewilderment.

'Sorry, sir. You'll see the joke in a minute.'

Alf Shaw, it emerged, had been in a distinctly grumpy mood. He was one of those aggressively plain men of the union movement, much given to phrases like 'I speak as I find'. He had been, he said, well pissed off at being endlessly mucked about by the police. He had cut Gifford short when he began to ask questions about his relationship with Sir Nicholas, and asked if an alibi for Gladys Bradley's murder would let him out of the whole business. Gifford had replied cautiously that it probably would, and Shaw had, with considerable embarrassment, provided a story which accounted fully for the missing two hours of Tuesday which had kept him on the list.

'But he told Romford on the phone that he had spent the time walking round Hyde Park planning a speech.'

'I know, but he had made that up on the spur of the moment because his secretary was in the room when he took the call. He'd thought of ringing back with the real story, but had decided to wait until he saw you.'

'What was the truth?'

Gifford stopped to savour his revelation. 'He'd been on a protracted visit to Nixon's lady friend—Sally.'

'I don't believe it. It's too much of a coincidence.'

'It's not really, sir. Shaw says she's very popular with top people. They're very nervous about illicit sex since the Lambton and Jellicoe scandal, and Sally is known to be very discreet. It's one of her main attractions. It seems that good mates recommend her to each other like a tailor or a restaurant. Shaw says he heard about her from some nob in the CBI he got drunk with at a conference.'

'And Sally confirmed his story?'

'Absolutely. And I'm sure she's telling the truth. She's got a very nice number going at the moment. She'd be mad to louse it up by lying to the police.'

'Tell me about her.'

Gifford had been greatly struck by Sally's charms, though he added hastily that she was way out of his bracket. She had a luxurious flat in Knightsbridge with a concealed separate entrance, and she provided her clients not just with sex and guaranteed secrecy, but also, if they wanted it, with food, drink and companionship. She had explained that she was a university graduate who had failed to get a decent job and had given considerable thought to finding a career in which she could meet interesting people and also make a lot of money.

'What was her degree in?'

'Sociology,' chuckled Gifford.

They turned around to walk back the way they had come.

'Well, I suppose she's putting it to more practical use than a lot of her contemporaries.'

'Too right. She says she wanted to do social work, but felt she'd be wasted on problem families. She's very pretty and enjoys conversation and says she provides a terrific social service helping important people to relax from the strain of their work. Half the time, she says, they don't even want sex. They're too knackered. All they want is sympathetic female companionship.'

'What's wrong with their wives?' asked Milton self-righteously.

'She says a lot of them suffer from broken or failing marriages, either because they've risen fast and the little woman can't keep up with them, or because they spend so much time away from home they become like strangers. She'd make you feel sorry for them, sir. Says they've very little fun.'

Milton remembered what Amiss had said about the demands made on ministers' time. He'd even repeated it himself to that creep from the Sunday rag. It all made sense. Most of the fellows in top jobs wouldn't have the opportunity to chase girls in the usual way. Too time-consuming. And they could hardly all be expected to remain celibate.

'It's a pity the Commissioner's going to have to hear about this,' he said. 'He'll have the vice-squad on to her straight away.'

'I don't think they'll get anywhere with Sally. She's thought all that out too. She doesn't charge her clients. Says they're all friends and it's her business if she's a bit promiscuous.'

'But money must come into it somewhere.'

'No. She never takes money. They give her presents. Jewellery mostly. Or pictures. There's one that gives her postage stamps. It's understood between them that these are given mostly as birthday or Christmas presents. They're nearly all regulars, you see. She says she only loses clients when they fall in love or lose their jobs and can't afford the presents any more.'

'Did she give you names?'

'I didn't press her on that. She insisted that she never told any of them about each other. We left it that we'd come back to her for names if we couldn't find out any other way who tipped off the newspaper.'

'We won't need them now. I'm certain Sir Nicholas was the source. How long had Nixon been seeing her?'

'She was very reluctant to talk about that, but she's a sensible girl and didn't want to get on the wrong side of us. It's been about three years, apparently. Since a couple of years after his divorce.'

'Did she say much about him?'

'Just that he used to come on Sunday nights when he was in London. She says he's one of her favourites. Called him a sweetie and said he couldn't possibly murder anyone.'

Milton hoped Sally was right. He wasn't so sure himself. Much as he liked Nixon, there was no point in pretending. If he had discovered that Sir Nicholas had blown the gaff on his idyllic evenings with Sally he would have had a bloody good reason to blow his top and despatch him on the spot. Square one again: any of these people might have killed Sir Nicholas, but it would have taken a very callous one to dispose of Gladys.

He caught himself falling back into his usual circular argument and checked it. His watch showed that it was now 2.20 and he had to try to get hold of Amiss before seeing Nixon. He thanked Gifford and set off for the short walk to the House of Commons.

Chapter Thirty-five

Milton sat in the resplendent lobby and waited for the Commons policeman to locate Amiss. He had taken the precaution of thinking up a question about Sir Nicholas's movements on Friday, which would serve as an excuse for seeing Amiss. The policeman returned alone.

'I'm sorry, sir, but Mr Amiss is with some other colleagues giving some last-minute briefing to the Secretary of State. I can call him out if it's urgent.'

'No, that's quite all right. I've got plenty of time. When do you expect him to be free?'

'Well, sir, I could ask him to come and see you when they've finished. Otherwise he'll be going straight into the Officials' Box and won't be free until the Secretary of State has finished his half hour of questions.'

Milton thought for a moment. It would be manifestly unreasonable to take Amiss away at a time like this. Whatever he had to say could keep until after Question Time. They could have a couple of minutes together before Milton went to see Nixon. Besides, he had never seen the House in session. It would be interesting to see Nixon at work in the place where he had made his reputation. Interesting, too, to see how he was bearing up publicly when he must be under considerable private strain.

'It's not urgent, Constable. It can keep until he's free. Can I watch from the Public Gallery?'

'The Strangers' Gallery, sir,' said the officer automatically. 'Certainly, sir. Come with me.'

Milton followed him into a narrow corridor, up a flight of stairs and into a small gallery already filled with tourists. Didn't any of the British ever come and watch their legislators at work? He supposed they waited until the tourist season was over—whenever that was. As far as he could see these days, the streets were packed with foreigners nearly all the year around. You couldn't really blame Londoners for turning xenophobic. There were times when he found himself wanting to rant furiously at the holiday-makers who filled the pubs round Westminster full to overflowing at times when the native population only wanted a quick drink and a sandwich in peace.

The constable produced a seat in the front row of the gallery by the simple expedient of making a crowd of Americans squash up grumblingly. The matron of the group shot a look of deep resentment at Milton and addressed her rumbling complaints to her mate in a rather piercing *sotto voce*. Milton took no notice: he was far too occupied in trying to spot familiar faces on the green leather benches of the amphitheatre which lay beneath his feet. It was filling up fast. Nixon was going to have a pretty good audience by Commons standards. Milton knew that M.P.s didn't turn up in the Chamber in large numbers unless they were expecting a bit of excitement. Hadn't he read that there were nothing like enough seats for a full turn-out and that on special occasions there was standing-room only? It seemed an eccentric way to run things, but presumably it all added to the excitement to have them jostling with each other on the staircases which led up from the floor of the Chamber to the ascending benches.

Milton had already identified half the front bench and a sprinkling of the Shadow Cabinet when Harvey Nixon came into the Chamber and took his seat in the front row on the left. Wells followed him in a minute later and took up a place a few rows back. Did that mean the Prime Minister had had the balls to sack him or that he had seen fit to resign? Milton suddenly spotted an even more familiar face. Amiss was sitting in a sort of enclosure directly opposite him. Of course, the Officials' Box. Milton strained his eyes to see who was with him. He recognized Sanders and Parkinson easily, but there seemed to be a couple of others he didn't know. What was Amiss doing here, anyway, if he was just a Private Secretary? Weren't the civil servants there to pass briefing notes on their areas of responsibility when their ministers were in trouble? Sanders must have brought him along to keep him company. But wasn't Sanders too elevated to be sitting in a box along with his juniors? Parkinson, Milton remembered, was a mere Assistant Secretary. Presumably there was some reason to expect trouble—probably over Wells's article.

Milton was trying vainly to catch Amiss's eye when a sonorous voice emitting from beneath a flowing wig indicated to the Honourable Members that it was time they got down to business. The Americans seemed mystified by his appearance. They began an audible discussion about the historical reasons for wearing silly clothes and headgear, which went on with singular disregard for the solemnity of the prayers which opened proceedings, and for the bits of miscellaneous and incomprehensible business which kept the M.P.s occupied until 2.45. To Milton's relief they were then threatened by a constable with immediate eviction unless they shut up instantly. The Speaker announced the name of a member, who rose and said unhelpfully, 'Number 1, Sir'. Mystique was all very well, thought Milton, but it was a bit thick if they were all going to talk in code. It reminded him of the old story about the convicts who numbered their stock of jokes because they knew them so well and used to fall about laughing when the number of their favourite was called out. No laughter this time—his timing was all off.

Things became clearer when Nixon began to speak. He obviously was privy to the content of question number 1. He was talking glibly about the non-viability of a project designed to recycle glass in Wales. When he concluded, the burly Welshman, whose question had triggered off this response, rose and asked a real question which indicated his distress at the government's hard-hearted lack of concern for his constituents' employment prospects. Milton thought that Nixon handled the answer well. He seemed hardly to have to consult his notes before he delivered a stream of facts designed to prove that the Welshman's electorate had been doing very nicely for government-assisted jobs. They had apparently been fortunate enough recently to have two electronics factories sited within their area. The Welshman wasn't appeased. That, he pointed out, was all very well, but they provided employment mainly for women. What was Nixon doing to provide jobs for the unemployed steel workers who would be ideally suited to work in a glass-recycling plant? Could he tell the House exactly how many of them had been made redundant during the previous six months and how many had by now found jobs?

Nixon seemed to hesitate as he flicked quickly through his notes. He looked over at the civil servants. Surely he must have the answer to that, Milton thought. It was inconceivable that the officials responsible would have neglected to provide the answer to such an obvious follow-up question. Milton scrutinized the occupants of the enclosure and saw Parkinson scribbling on a piece of paper. Nixon began to answer the question in measured tones. He was playing for time, Milton assumed, by giving annual statistics of unemployment, but he clearly didn't have the six-monthly figures, or if he did he couldn't find them. Presumably, if there was some particular significance in the six-monthly figures he wouldn't get off with that. Parkinson must be busy supplementing the information.

Milton looked again at the Box to see how Parkinson would get the note to his minister. He could hardly leap over the partition which marked his separateness from the Members. There must be a minion to do that. He saw a tail-coated attendant approach him and hover as he waited for the note to be proffered. Parkinson didn't seem to be coming up with the goods. He had stopped writing and was leaning back in his seat clutching his stomach. Nixon was stringing out his answer with a flood of statistics about cost per job, redeployment successes and the government's record in job creation during its term of office.

Milton wasn't listening. He was growing increasingly concerned about the kerfuffle in the Box. Parkinson had slipped off his seat and Sanders and Amiss were bent over him. The sweat was standing out on Milton's brow. He leaped from his seat and rushed out of the gallery to find someone to take him through the labyrinth of corridors to the back of the Box. He was praying as he ran down the stairs. He didn't know if it was for Parkinson or himself.

Chapter Thirty-six

By the time Milton reached them, Sanders, Amiss and a couple of attendants had carried Parkinson into the corridor. They were standing by helplessly. The carpet was spattered with vomit and the stains of uncontrollable diarrhoea. Cries of agony issued from the convulsed face below them. The horror of it had set their faces in rigid lines of sympathetic pain. As two men in uniform ran up with a stretcher and a medical kit, Milton led the two civil servants away. They would have trouble enough in banishing the image of this from their minds without seeing any more.

He was badly shaken himself, but he was lucky in having work to do. He made the necessary arrangements for officers to follow Parkinson to hospital and be ready to pass on to Milton's temporary headquarters at the House any news on how he was progressing, or of anything he might say.

He was quickly found a room and he called in Sanders and Amiss to question them on Parkinson's sudden illness. It was as he had feared. Parkinson had complained of indigestion and dehydration, had been perspiring heavily, and had shown signs of intensified symptoms as he sat in the Box. The convulsions had started when he fell to the floor. Sanders had tried earlier to persuade him to leave the House and go home or get medical treatment, but Parkinson had insisted that he would be all right. Milton felt sick when he realized that the poor fellow was probably trying to prove himself in front of his new Permanent Secretary.

He chafed with impatience while he went through the motions of interviewing the others who had been sitting in the Officials' Box. They all told the same story. He gave himself a moment alone to ring the hospital. Maybe there was still a chance that this would prove to be simply a bad case of food poisoning. There wasn't. The doctor to whom he spoke was in no doubt. Parkinson was suffering from acute arsenic poisoning. Milton's worst suspicions were confirmed.

He made some more telephone calls to set enquiries in train, and then recalled Sanders and Amiss. He needed to know Parkinson's movements. They might be able to add something to the evidence others were now getting from his secretary and staff. All they knew, they said unhappily, was that Parkinson had had a working lunch with Nixon at about 1.30. There had been so much for Sanders and Nixon to talk about in relation to Wells's sacking that the Secretary of State hadn't been able to keep his late-morning appointment with Parkinson. It had been Nixon's idea that they should lunch together and go over the brief on the glass-recycling plant. All the civil servants had had ten minutes or so together with Nixon just before Question Time to clear up any problems that might have occurred to him.

Milton sat silently contemplating the obvious inference that Nixon had had an excellent opportunity to poison Parkinson. He sent a patiently waiting sergeant to question the canteen staff. He was about to dismiss Sanders and Amiss for the time being and call in Nixon, who had finished in the Chamber and was standing by to keep their appointment, when he caught sight of Amiss gesticulating at him from behind Sanders's back. Of course, he had wanted to see him about something. The message from Ann seemed to have come a long, long time ago. He called out as they were leaving the room.

'Excuse me, Mr Amiss, but something has come up about Sir Nicholas which you should be able to answer. Would you mind staying for a moment?'

Milton's mind wasn't on what Amiss was saying. All he could think of was what the next news from the hospital would be.

Surely they had got Parkinson in time? He couldn't be dying. Hadn't he suffered enough in his life not to deserve an appalling death like this? But then so had Gladys. This murderer probably didn't know or care about the kind of people he killed. He must be a savage. Gladys's death was mercifully quick, at least. Only a fiend would kill with arsenic.

He looked up dully at Amiss, who seemed to be talking about a missing appointments diary. It wasn't like Robert to witter on like this when there was something so much more urgent going on. His telephone rang.

'It's Pike, sir. I've had a couple of people at work checking alibis and Jenkins, Nigel Clark and Stafford are in the clear. They couldn't have seen Parkinson today. I can't get hold of Lady Clark and I'm still double-checking on Wells's movements.'

Milton closed his eyes and thought. Amiss hadn't started talking again. Shaw was out as well. That left two people who might have murdered Parkinson, unless of course someone had found a way of getting the poison to him indirectly or at an earlier date. Why? Why? Why? What could Parkinson possibly have known that would have made him a danger now? He was no Gladys, too confused to make sense of anything he had seen or heard. He was a trained scientist, for God's sake. But maybe he had been keeping quiet for a reason? Was it conceivable that that open relaxed man had been indulging in blackmail? If so, of whom? Wells? Fruitless. Wells didn't have either money or power. Nixon? He had some indirect power over Parkinson's career, and a little money. Lady Clark? She had money.

Pike rang again. 'Lady Clark and Mr Wells are in the clear also, sir, as far as today is concerned.'

He looked up at Amiss. 'I'm sorry, Robert. I can't talk to you now. I've got to see Nixon. He's not going to be able to explain his way out of this one, if I'm any judge. Apart from anything else, we've discovered that Sir Nicholas knew he was mixed up with a call-girl.'

'You've got to listen to me first, Jim.'

The phone rang again. This time it was from the hospital. Milton listened for a moment and hung up. 'Parkinson's dead, Robert.'

'But he can't be,' cried Amiss. 'I was sure he was the murderer.'

Chapter Thirty-seven

Amiss's argument was that the key to Gladys's murder lay in resolving the question of who had had an early Monday morning appointment with Sir Nicholas. Although Milton felt it was rather academic now, he had pulled himself together and accepted that, since Amiss wasn't a fool, he should do him the courtesy of listening. There was no harm in letting Nixon sweat for a few minutes longer. He followed and approved of the line of reasoning that had led Amiss to that conclusion.

Amiss had been able to check on Wells and Nixon easily. There was no problem in consulting their diaries and having a brief tangential chat with their staff. Nixon had unquestionably arrived back in London on the shuttle half an hour before the IGGY meeting. Wells had met his Private Secretary more than an hour before IGGY to go obsessively over the brief with him. Parkinson had been more of a problem. His secretary was extremely unapproachable and guarded her secrets jealously. Amiss couldn't think of any way of finding out about Parkinson's early-morning movements without looking suspiciously nosey. He had had a brainwave which he was now embarrassed about. He excused himself in advance by a sheepish admission that he had let his enthusiasm run away with him.

'What did you do?'

'I rang up his secretary—I knew he was out of the room—imitated your voice, gave your name, and said I was doing a routine check of the early-morning movements of everyone concerned in the case.'

Milton pulled himself back from the brink of rage. This was his ally, after all, whose enthusiasm had up until now been of incomparable value to the enquiry.

'And she said …?'

'That while there was nothing in his diary for Monday morning other than the IGGY meeting, he had been in unusually early. His coat was on the rack when she got in at 8.45. She didn't know where he'd been, but he had come back a few minutes later.'

'You're not trying to tell me that on the basis of this you concluded that he was a murderer?'

'Of course not. It wasn't enough in itself. But it tied in with something that Sanders consulted me about this morning which gave Parkinson a real and urgent motive for murdering Sir Nicholas.'

'Yes?'

'He was in line for the Under Secretaryship of a new division which needed a scientist-cum-administrator. Sanders wanted to know what I thought of him. He said he'd just been talking to the Personnel people about it and they were waiting for a recommendation from the Permanent Secretary. Sanders was well-disposed. Thought Parkinson hadn't had a fair deal from Sir Nicholas.'

'Would Parkinson have known he was in the running?'

'Not in the normal course of events. But Sanders said Sir Nicholas had known about it last Friday. Isn't it highly possible that he made an appointment with Parkinson for Monday morning to tell him he wouldn't recommend him?'

Milton tried to cast his mind back a few hours. Yes. Had he heard about this then he would have followed it up with alacrity. The big thing in Parkinson's favour all along had been his lack of an urgent motive. Knowing Sir Nicholas, there was every reason to believe that he would have wanted to raise Parkinson's hopes over the weekend, only to dash them on Monday morning. But that, as he told Amiss, was now entirely and eternally hypothetical, since both principals in the supposed conversations were unable to confirm it.

'Could he have committed suicide? Or intended just to make himself ill in order to draw suspicion away from himself?'

'You've had a taste of what arsenic poisoning does to someone, Robert. Do you really think it's likely anyone would commit suicide that way? And he was a scientist, don't forget. He wouldn't have given himself a fatal dose if he wanted to make himself ill. He'd have calculated it carefully. No. I'm afraid that while your theory would have seemed plausible this morning, it's not a runner now. Apart from anything else, can you explain why he should have committed suicide?'

'No,' said Amiss unhappily. 'But just for the sake of it, will you have someone check through his things here and in the office for a suicide note?'

'All right, Robert. I'll do that now. Will you tell Nixon I'll want him in a couple of minutes?'

The Assistant Commissioner burst through the door as Milton finished his call. It took a few minutes to bring him up-to-date about Nixon's possible new motive, the elimination of Alfred Shaw and the fact that, with the exception of Nixon, none of the suspects had had any contact with Parkinson that day.

'And you haven't arrested him yet?' he asked incredulously.

'I'm not one hundred per cent certain, sir. I was just going to question him again.'

'If you had questioned him earlier today Parkinson might be alive now. What possible reason can you have for holding back? Don't you realize that we're already likely to be accused of incompetence? We don't want a charge of giving special treatment to a government minister levelled against us as well.'

'There are three things worrying me, sir. First, why should Nixon have wanted to kill Parkinson? I can't think of a motive which will hold water. Second, why would he have been so incredibly stupid as to poison him over lunch and make himself the Number One suspect? ...'

'Blackmail and bravado,' said the A.C. crisply. 'What's the third?'

Milton tip-toed on egg-shells in putting forward Amiss's theory as if it were a long-shot of his own. He had difficulty in looking the A.C. in the eye as he mentioned having made a phone call to Parkinson's secretary. He concluded by mentioning he had organized a hunt for a suicide note.

'Rubbish,' said the A.C. 'You've been letting your imagination work overtime. Parkinson's been murdered by the same person who showed himself ready to take massive risks with his earlier killings. Let's get the bastard in and break him.'

Before you go back to the Yard and break me, thought Milton. He went out to find Nixon.

Chapter Thirty-eight

Nixon could do nothing except sit there and deny everything. No, Sir Nicholas hadn't said anything to him about Sally. He might have intended to, but Nixon had avoided him after the meeting. No, he hadn't murdered him. No, he hadn't murdered Gladys. No, he hadn't been blackmailed by Parkinson. Nor had Parkinson told him he knew anything about the earlier murders. No, he hadn't poisoned Parkinson. All he had done was buy him lunch out of the kindness of his heart.

Milton remained silent throughout the questioning. The A.C. had begun politely enough, but his patience was wearing thin by the end of half an hour of asking the same questions and getting the same answers. When the interim pathology report came through with the news that Parkinson had died from a dose of arsenic large enough to kill a horse, taken along with his lunch, the A.C. began to shout.

Nixon didn't respond. The frankness which had made Milton like him so much was not manifesting itself now. He just went on with simple denials. If he was guilty, thought Milton, he was probably taking the right line. The A.C. had insisted on making the interview formal; there was a sergeant present with a short-hand notebook taking down every word. Nixon hadn't asked for a solicitor, but he didn't need one. He was giving nothing away. Conversely, he certainly wasn't taking the right line if he was innocent. It was conceivable that a sufficiently articulate and open response to questions might at least have raised a few doubts in the A.C.'s mind—enough to hold him back from arresting Nixon on the spot.

Amiss, meanwhile, had spent a long time sitting with Sanders. He was impressed by how Sanders, distressed though he clearly was, had risen above his ordeal. He had begun to work on some of the papers in his briefcase, and he even found the heart to enquire how Question Time had gone. Reasonably well, it turned out. Officials were supposed to be invisible, but even such a well-established convention hadn't survived the sight of one of them being carried out *in extremis*. There was also probably a feeling that poor old Harvey had been left at an unfair disadvantage. He had been let off lightly, and the row over Wells's sacking had been extremely half-hearted—apparently to Wells's patent dissatisfaction. Even the P.M.'s Question Time had been subdued. Amiss had been struck by the fact that, although Nixon had hurried out to see Parkinson as soon as he had finished, Wells hadn't even bothered to enquire about him.

Amiss wasted some time trying to think of some way in which Wells might have murdered Parkinson. Poisoned chocolates sent through the post seemed as unlikely as doctored decanters. No, Nixon was going to be arrested and the resultant explosion of shit was going to finish off the government. Nixon hadn't a chance. With a sexual scandal on top of his other motive, the fact that the evidence against him was purely circumstantial was unlikely to stop a jury finding him guilty.

Amiss's mind went obsessively over and over the case he had built up against Parkinson. What were the flaws? In the murder of Sir Nicholas, only the same one that applied to any other suspect. He'd have had to take an immense risk. The killing of Gladys after such a long delay was a poser, whoever was responsible, but admittedly even more so if Parkinson had done it. There was a fair chance that nothing would ever have come to light about the Monday morning meeting. As against that, Parkinson's motive for the original murder was now better than anyone else's. Any of them might have killed Sir Nicholas for revenge, but only Parkinson could have done it for gain.

Hadn't he overstressed to Milton his conviction that his career was beyond rescue?

Amiss was pacing up and down the corridor. He saw Sanders shoot him a sympathetic look. He sat down beside him again and resisted the temptation to confide his worries. Sanders suddenly gathered up his papers and shoved them back into his briefcase. He looked at Amiss.

'They're going to arrest Nixon, don't you think?'

'I'm afraid it looks like it, Douglas.'

'I can't really believe it. What are we supposed to do now? It's a friend he needs, not two impotent bystanders. He hasn't even got his Private Secretary. Where the hell is he?'

Amiss was taken aback, but comforted once again at finding that it was possible to rise to the top in the civil service and keep a heart.

'Nixon sent him back to the office. He said he didn't want to keep him hanging about all afternoon.'

At this further example of Nixon's courtesy towards his staff, even in his greatest hour of trial, Sanders fell into a depressed silence. They had both been sitting there gazing at the wall for several minutes when the door of the room in which Nixon was being grilled opened, and Milton stepped out. He was expressionless.

'Mr Nixon is accompanying us to the Yard to assist us further with our enquiries, sir,' he said, addressing Sanders. 'Could someone go to his room and retrieve his coat? Will you, Mr Amiss? And Mr Sanders, I should like your advice on how we can get out of this building without having to run the gauntlet of the press. I understand they've gathered in force outside.'

So that was that. As Amiss began the walk towards Nixon's office he reflected that Nixon was now undeniably finished. Even if another murderer was found at a later stage, the very fact that Nixon had been for a time the prime suspect would lose him his seat as well as his ministerial office. His seat was marginal, and there would always be enough people swayed by the belief that there was 'no smoke without fire' to make them change their votes. There was no stopping the press. Whatever back exit Sanders found, some of the boys would be hovering round. They'd probably even manage to meet the deadline for the last edition of the evening paper.

Amiss found Nixon's coat without difficulty and began his trek back. He was still turning over in his mind the Parkinson theory. It was obvious that Milton's instructions to search for a suicide note had yielded nothing. Whatever he'd done, Parkinson was too decent to kill himself and leave others to take the blame. The whole notion was a non-starter, and the sooner he came to terms with it the better. It was the height of arrogance to assume that because it was his theory it must be right. Why shouldn't it be Nixon, anyway? Kindness and courtesy could mask viciousness; they could be no more than a façade. And what viciousness Nixon must have shown to do that to Parkinson. A shudder ran through Amiss as he thought of his last sight of the man. He had been terrified from the first moment he had seen him clasp his hand to his stomach and his face contort. It had taken only a moment. One minute he had been writing, the next …

Amiss stopped at the entrance to the corridor he was making for. He saw the small group awaiting him expectantly at the far end. He dropped Nixon's coat, turned and ran.

A debate was in progress as he tumbled into the Officials' Box. The Secretary of State for Energy was on his feet and was disconcerted by the noise which Amiss made as he pushed colleagues out of the way and scrabbled on the floor. Amiss didn't hear the reproving tones of the Speaker as he called for silence, nor the agitated voices of colleagues begging him to quieten down.

He found it lying under Parkinson's seat. As he opened up the crumpled piece of paper he gave a whoop of delight that wrung further bleats of consternation from his colleagues. Ignoring them, he ran from the Box.

Thursday Evening

Chapter Thirty-nine

'And what did it say?' Ann Milton asked Amiss, fascinated.

'That after Sir Nicholas had told him on Friday that he was thinking of recommending him for the Under-Secretaryship, he realized how much promotion did matter to him after all. Then, at the meeting they had arranged for early Monday morning, Sir Nicholas laughed at him and said he'd see he stayed an Assistant Secretary for ever. After the IGGY meeting, Sir Nicholas looked over at him and sneered. Parkinson stood trying to make conversation for several minutes and then went out looking for him. He saw Sir Nicholas disappearing into the lavatory, followed him in, saw he was alone, went back for the sculpture and hit him with it.'

'And Gladys?'

'He said he didn't mean to kill her. He went up to find out if she remembered the Monday-morning meeting, because if she did he was going to tell Jim some story to explain it away. She didn't say anything about it, but told him that Lady Clark and Nigel had just taken away those sculptures of Sir Nicholas's that she didn't like—those ones, she said, that looked just like the one she had seen him pick up outside the conference room on Monday morning.'

'She didn't make the connection at all?'

'Hadn't taken in the full story when we told her, I suppose.'

'So he killed her on the spur of the moment?'

'Yes, and took the diary for good measure. He suffered for his impulse, though. He thought about giving himself up but couldn't face the thought of life imprisonment. He got hold of some arsenic—painful death, expiation of some sort—but he couldn't nerve himself to take it. Then today his secretary told him that Jim had rung up to enquire about his movements on Monday morning and he concluded that it wouldn't be long before he was arrested. That's why he took the poison at lunch.'

'But how could he possibly get all this down on paper?'

'Oh, it wasn't connected prose. Scribbled notes really. It was dreadful to read. The handwriting was shaky and he ended up scrawling "I'm sorry".'

'Why did he stay on for Question Time?'

'Too ill to leave, I expect. Anyway the note implied that he was making a public statement of remorse by dying before an audience.'

'The poor devil,' said Ann. 'He must have been in more than one kind of agony.'

'I haven't got too much sympathy, Ann,' said Milton. 'Harvey Nixon was in agony too, and if Robert hadn't had that brainwave he'd probably have ended up serving a life sentence. Parkinson can't have been thinking straight to write a suicide note that could so easily be missed.'

'Well, of course he wasn't thinking straight,' said Amiss. 'It's my guess he was intending to hand the note to the attendant to give to Nixon, but the convulsions hit him before he expected them. At least you've got to admit that he atoned pretty comprehensively. He must have had a very tender conscience to put himself through that.'

'Oh, I know you're right, Robert. It's just that I feel ill every time I think how close we came to missing it. Nixon and I both owe you an enormous debt.'

'Nixon's been very nice about it. Full of relief and gratitude. Sanders seemed very chuffed too, and not just about Nixon's innocence, either. Parkinson's suicide means the papers won't get hold of the story of Sir Nicholas's little japes, which is a load off Sanders's mind. He's also relieved at the discovery that his Private Secretary hasn't gone mad.'

'So were we all,' laughed Milton. 'When you dropped Nixon's coat and scrammed like that there were raised eyebrows all round. I was the only one who nurtured the hope that you'd suddenly had an inspiration.'

'What happened when he arrived back with the note?' asked Ann.

'He came running up shouting "I've found it, I've found it". Had some difficulty in getting us to stop and listen. The A.C. was set on getting Nixon off to the Yard as quickly as possible. Two minutes later and he'd have had to throw himself under the front wheels of the car.'

'What's going to happen to Nixon now?'

'I think he'll probably have to hang on in his job for a while,' said Amiss. 'Otherwise it'll look as if the P.M. thinks there was something shady about the whole business. Still, I don't suppose he'll mind that too much. He's in a state of euphoria at the moment.'

'But isn't that newspaper going to blow the story of his visits to the call-girl?'

'No, it's not,' said Milton. 'She rang Gifford at the Yard this afternoon and said they're killing it. Apparently the proprietor is a friend of hers.' He'd been saving that, and he wasn't disappointed in the reaction. They drank the lady's health.

'Well, it seems to be a happy ending all round—except for the Parkinsons. We're even going to be able to go to Paris on Saturday,' Ann beamed.

'Lucky old you,' said Amiss dispiritedly. 'I've got the twin delights facing me of Sir Nicholas's funeral tomorrow and Gladys's on Saturday. It's not fair that you're escaping all that.'

'I'm going to need that break,' said Milton. 'This has been the most intellectually exhausting case I've ever had. I'd have given up hope days ago if it hadn't been for you.'

'Come now, Jim. I spent a lot of the time muddying the waters with information that proved to be totally irrelevant.'

'Well, yes, but even all the irrelevant information helped me personally. When the A.C. got over his embarrassment with

Nixon he congratulated me warmly on having handled the case so well. He made much of the brilliant way I'd conducted the interviews, and, as a bonus, the way my telephone call to Parkinson's secretary had flushed him out. It was all very embarrassing really, taking the credit for your cleverness.'

'Thanks, but I don't think many of your colleagues would have thought of recruiting me. I wouldn't have lifted a finger to help if it hadn't been for that—and more specifically if you hadn't agreed to that exchange-of-information clause. I knew it was a big risk for you—there's enough in common between our working environments, so I couldn't fail to know it. That's when I started to like you. I still don't know how far you were throwing yourself on my mercy and how much of it was insidious manipulation, but it worked. If you hadn't told me day by day the way the investigation was going, I'd never have given a second thought to the missing appointments diary when Phil started complaining about it.'

'Oh, yes, Phil. That reminds me, did you know I met him at lunchtime today? Of course not, he won't have told you—I didn't leave my name.'

'He told me all right, Jim,' said Amiss, chuckling. 'He sussed out who you were. Said some senior pig had been looking for me.'

'How the hell did he know?' said Milton in a hurt tone. 'I take great pains to avoid looking like a policeman.'

'Sorry, Jim. All I can tell you is that he claimed you smelled like one.'

When Ann had finished laughing at her discomfited husband she turned to Amiss, serious again. 'But have you solved the real mystery of the whole affair—what Sir Nicholas was up to?'

'Well, I haven't worked out why he did what he did, but I'm morally certain that it was an elaborate way of committing suicide. Let's go through the story now. You're a psychologist of sorts. I knew him well enough. Jim's a copper, as any fool can smell, and he's met all the principals. There are all sorts of contradictions when you look at the people he hated and the ways he decided to get at them.'

Chapter Forty

'Shall we take it chronologically?' said Amiss. 'I mean as far back as we can go. We know from Lady Clark that Sir Nicholas began to change character in his first few years in the civil service—mainly, it seems, as a result of various personal disappointments he suffered around then—having to give up politics, the various miscarriages and her illnesses. The first question is, was he fundamentally a nasty piece of work whose true nature asserted itself when times became hard? Or were the problems so distressing to him that they affected his mental balance?'

'I don't think we know enough about him to say,' said Ann. 'A fundamentally decent person could react the way he did initially, just withdrawing into himself and putting all his energy into his work. It's what came later that suggests an evil streak.'

'Well, presumably his failure to get on well with his only child helped to increase his feeling of isolation.'

'We're talking about a highly intelligent, rational man here,' said Milton. 'He brought most of his isolation on himself. It wasn't the fault of Lady Clark or his colleagues that he became so distant in personal relationships.'

'Right,' said Ann. 'But he may have found himself caught in a vicious circle. People can deliberately cut themselves off from others and yet feel hurt that no one makes overtures of friendship or love. They're driven further into themselves and can even develop a sort of persecution mania—a conviction that others are lined up against them.'

'It was a funny kind of persecution mania that led him to persecute others,' said Milton.

'On the contrary. Hurt often makes people turn against those they think are responsible for making them unhappy. The deeper the hurt gets, the harder it is even to contemplate the fact that it might be self-inflicted.'

'But he doesn't seem to have been trying to hurt his wife or son,' said Amiss. 'What Lady Clark has described was in Nigel's case just misguided attention, and in her own simply impatience and a touch of contempt. Applying high standards. Lots of fathers and husbands behave like that. No, what bothers me is why he became so obviously vicious eight years ago when he began his persecution of Parkinson. I can't see any reason why he should have hated him. After all, they had been friends for a long time.'

'No,' said Ann, 'I can't think of any reason for that either. Unless it was jealousy. Maybe he began to hate Parkinson for being so handsome and successful—even happy. Lost all capacity to enjoy his old friend's personal progress, got guilty about it, and set about destroying the source of his guilt. Jim?'

'Makes a rough kind of sense. But why continue the persecution for so long—I mean, once he'd scotched Parkinson's career, why go for total destruction? Anyway, there doesn't seem to be any evidence that he hated anyone else in the way he hated Parkinson—until recently, that is. Sanders talked about him having gradually become more and more difficult to work with, but there's been no suggestion that he was anything other than indiscriminately malicious.'

'Until he started on Nixon a couple of years ago,' Ann broke in. 'From what we've heard about that his hatred was pretty carefully directed.'

'But Nixon is a thoroughly nice bloke. What could he possibly have done to merit such a degree of malice?'

'I think I understand that, Jim,' said Amiss. 'Nixon's incompetence seemed to annoy Sir Nicholas personally. I think he was trying to show him up as someone who didn't deserve to be in the job.'

'I'll buy that. He could have convinced himself that he was acting quite properly in making Nixon's life difficult. And his reasons for disliking Wells are pretty obvious too. Remember your reaction to him, darling.'

'I can't blame him for that,' said Amiss. 'His view of Wells was shared by most of us, and until last week he didn't behave towards him outrageously. He just made life a bit more difficult for him. We all dreamed of scuppering Wells—Sir Nicholas had the opportunity, once he'd forsaken all sense of official duty.'

'Right,' said Milton. 'So the crucial changes in him seem to go back twenty-nine, eight and two years. First a distancing of himself from everyone, then the beginning of a long-drawn-out campaign to destroy Parkinson and finally a consistent attempt to make Nixon's life a misery. Disappointment, jealousy-cum-guilt, and contempt, respectively.'

'Right,' said Amiss. 'It was as a part of that that he started to follow Nixon to try and get some dirt on him. Notifying the journalist about his visits to the call-girl was a logical step. But what about the hiring of the private detective to get the goods on his family? What prompted that?'

'He must have been completely twisted by then. Some psychologists might say that, having noticed they were unusually happy, and happiness having become the enemy, he decided to have it investigated.'

'So the discovery that they both owed their new happiness to other people turned him suicidal?' Amiss had been working for this wretch for eighteen months. He pushed his plate aside in disgust.

'But why didn't he take it out on them?' Milton was no more comfortable with Ann's theory. 'After all, he could have made terrific scenes about betrayal and deception by both of them. Wouldn't that have been the normal thing to do?'

'We're not talking about normality, Jim,' said Amiss. 'We're talking about Sir Nicholas. The only conclusion I can come to is that he lost all interest in living when he found out that his family didn't need him any more, and he decided to stir the shit in all possible directions and provoke someone into killing him.'

'But how could he be sure someone *would* kill him?'

'He couldn't.' An idea flashed into Amiss's mind. 'But what if he had a contingency plan to commit suicide if nobody obliged him? Must have. Otherwise, why would he have sent the note to the Yard about his wife and Martin Jenkins? I expect he was going to make the suicide look like murder in order to get one of those poor devils locked up for it.'

'You're reading too much into that, Robert. If there had been no murder we would simply have ignored such a note. It would have been filed away with all the other cranky tip-offs we get every day. It seems to me he was fighting off boredom with Russian Roulette.'

'No, Jim. I think Robert's right. He would have had nothing to live for except disgrace and loneliness. He must have been preparing himself for death. It's a strange way to go about it, though. Most people try to make peace at the end, not war. I presume he didn't believe in an after-life.'

'I've no idea what he believed in,' sighed Amiss. 'We didn't go in for conversations like that. He obviously must have had a pretty bleak view of the universe.'

'I can understand—although with some difficulty—what made him act so maliciously during his last few days,' said Ann. 'What makes my blood run cold is the thought that his spitefulness would extend to wanting to drive any of his victims—including his son—to murder. Maybe we should take the charitable view and conclude that he had simply gone insane. The alternative is too appalling to contemplate.'

'We'll never know,' said Milton, 'but from what I've learned about Sir Nicholas, my feeling is that he knew what he was doing and would have been delighted at the outcome. I think you're both being sentimental in talking about lovelessness and all that sort of thing. He was a vicious bastard who had lost interest in living and wanted to make other people pay for it. We could speculate forever. Let's order another round and drink to Robert's success in ensuring at least that we didn't add to Sir Nicholas's posthumous fun by pinning his murder on the wrong man. Let's also make a resolution to forget about Sir Nicholas and devote our next evening together—which I hope won't be too far distant—to more uplifting subjects. And better food.'

Friday Morning

Chapter Forty-one

''Ere you are,' said Phil, dropping a file in front of Amiss. 'You wanted to see this today.'

Amiss looked at the title on the front. '"Retrospection"? What the hell is this? I've never seen it before.'

'Must of done. There's a note in the diary sayin' you're s'posed to have it today.'

Amiss shrugged. Maybe he had forgotten about it. Noting in the diary that something should be looked at on some specified date in the future often meant that it had been too boring to contemplate when first seen and could better be faced at another time. 'Retrospection.' Probably some tedious analysis of the genesis of some policy or other. At least there wasn't much in it. He'd have more than enough time to read it before setting off with Sanders to say a public goodbye to his lunatic old boss.

The envelope pinned to the inside of the file was addressed to him, and when Amiss saw the handwriting he went cold. He tore a page inside as he opened it. The signature to the letter held no surprises; the date did. Sir Nicholas had written to him the previous Monday. Below the date he had written '6.00 a.m.'

'My dear Robert,' it began. Amiss rubbed his eyes at this unaccustomed friendliness.

> If my plans work out correctly, you will receive this four
> days after my death. You will, I imagine, be surprised that
> I have chosen to write to you. My reason will probably

surprise you even more. There is no one else about whom I now care enough to offer an explanation of my actions in recent weeks. Nor is there anyone else for whom such an explanation may be useful. I hope that what I am going to tell you may help you, in the future, to maintain that sense of perspective which I have at times sought, but never found.

You will almost certainly be surprised to learn that I have an affection for you. I realize that my conduct to you during the time you have worked for me has given no hint of this. That is because I have long been incapable of showing any emotions other than contempt or dislike. There has been within me for years a devil which has made me unable to see any of those around me as anything other than unworthy of positive feelings. You have been an exception. You have seemed to lack the venality, stupidity, unjustified arrogance or unwarranted ambition which I see all around me. I have liked in you what people once liked in me—intelligence, honesty, humanity and a sense of the ridiculous. You will counter by saying that there are many people we know who share those qualities. I can say only that if that is true, my perceptions of others have become too warped to enable me to perceive their virtues. It may well be that I am seeing industriousness as careerism, warmth as obsequiousness, silence as cowardice. I don't know and it is too late now to find out.

I intend to kill myself today, either by provoking my own murder or by taking cyanide, a small supply of which I have concealed at the back of the drawer in which I intend to place this file. If it is murder, the police will have found a sufficiency of suspects. If it is suicide, I intend that they will be equally well provided for, as I intend to call in to see me this evening—and one by one—as many as possible of those at whom my venom is presently directed, leaving each of them alone for a moment or two in the room with an open sherry decanter, from which I will later drink with fatal consequence. It will be quite in character, given the conversations I intend to engineer, for me not to offer them a drink.

Amiss got up and went over to the filing cabinet. A moment later, with a small bottle in his hand, he continued reading his letter.

> My intention is to ensure that a small number of people have a bad few days, and that the circumstances which have led them to become suspects be brought into the open. I don't know what you will have heard of the investigation by the time you read this letter. You will certainly be aware of what I have done to bring about the downfall of Nixon and Wells. Unless I am very lucky in the circumstances of my demise you may not know that I have also sought to embarrass my wife, her lover, my son, Richard Parkinson and Archibald Stafford.
>
> You will be wondering first, why I should have decided to bring about my own death, and second, why I should do so with such apparent malevolence. The answer to the first question is that I can see no point whatsoever in going on with a life so arid as mine. As for the second, I consider these people to deserve whatever I can do to them.
>
> I believed, you see, in my youth, that I had qualities that would make it possible for me to make a valuable contribution to society. In adverse circumstances I got to Oxford, and I was successful there. I believed that I could become a political figure of significance and that, through the exercise of energy and ability, I could change the face of this country. That that was a foolish ambition I now recognize. In a society as undisciplined as ours, all leaders are powerless. Over the years I have watched the idealism go out of politicians as they come to understand that the realities of democracy make them prisoners of the greed of their electorate. Yet, foolish as I may have been

as a young man, at least I had a sense of purpose, which made my life seem worthwhile. Perhaps if I had been lucky and obtained political power early I might have adjusted to its constraints and been a useful and well-balanced citizen, instead of the sterile and repellent creature I have now become. It is difficult to say. Sometimes I think that frustration and resentment at the direction my life has taken have been paramount in changing my outlook on life—in other words, that I am bitter because—and only because—I see myself as a failure. At other times I see my contempt for the way we run our society as the only intellectually valid point of view. Almost certainly, both these elements are present in some proportion. I have at all times sought a philosophical basis for my position. I have read—almost exclusively, and increasingly desperately in recent years—about people who have brought change, and about the beliefs that led them to act as they did.

My researches have been as sterile as my life. I can believe in no religion. What God could so ordain things that our world should be dominated by a species so feeble and vicious? And what philosophy has ever proved to be more than mental masturbation or a failure in practice? Perhaps Nietzsche came closest. He at least recognized that an intelligent élite should control events—not a collection of fools whose only merit is their ability to hoodwink the mindless populace. Even his philosophy, though, did nothing in practice save provide the basis for a distorted justification of the nastiest régimes I have seen in operation in my lifetime. No. I have accepted that it was naïve ever to think that special abilities fit one for the improvement of mankind. They are a curse and not, as I once thought, a blessing. They enable one to see the truth about the human condition, without enabling one to do anything to improve it.

Amiss got up, made himself a cup of coffee and stole a cigarette from Phil. He felt a deep depression flooding through him.

You will point out that gifted people do reach positions of power from which they can affect the course of history. I would point you towards the far greater numbers of them who get no such opportunity, but spend their lives looking wonderingly at the mess their idiotic contemporaries are making of things, and towards those whose successful efforts are spat upon, before they are cold in their graves, by their mediocre successors. You may point out also that one should make the best of the situation in which one finds oneself—that like you, one should at least attempt to be reasonably efficient and humane within one's constraints. You are right if you believe this. That is exactly what I should have done. I could have made at least this department a happier and more effective organization. I did not because I could never lose sight of the opportunities I had lost, and I felt only contempt for the tiny contribution I would be allowed to make. That is why I have chosen to write this to you. Do not take the same destructive path. If you ever find that dissatisfaction with the work you are doing has taken a grip on you, change your life drastically, even at the expense of those of whom you are fond. You will always have in me a prime example of how discontent can lead to hatred, not only of other people but of oneself.

It is self-hatred which has led me to decide to kill myself. I should have done it years ago, but there lurked within me always a stupidly tenacious belief that my *Weltanschauung* might change with promotion for more recognition of my abilities—promotion to more important departments—had not my uselessness been made clear to me by developments in my private life. Only the week before last I found that my wife, whom I trusted and had once loved, found a rabble-rousing leader of the great unwashed more worthy of her affections than me, and that my son, for whom I have always had a deep if unexpressed love, had become a queer. My knowledge of popular psychology leads me to assume that that was in some way my fault. I realized that they would be better off without me, and that I could not in any case bear the ignominy of seeing them desert me. Were I a better person, I should have taken a quiet way out, so causing them and everyone else the least possible distress, but the cancer of bitterness within me does not allow me to do what I perceive to be the weak and apologetic thing.

You will therefore see that my motives for trying to involve my family and Martin Jenkins in my death are those of simple jealousy and the desire for revenge. You will also probably understand by now why I have so carefully set out to implicate Nixon and Wells. The first I despise profoundly. He has no right to be in the position he is in. He has certainly no right to expect one of my abilities to strive to save him from public recognition of his undoubted stupidity. Stupidity. Worse than cupidity? Wells is able—I cannot deny that. But he is foul. He has no thought of anything but his own preferment. I consider my efforts to destroy the careers of the two of them to be in the public interest. Those efforts have too the virtue of bringing them to grief because of their own failings. It was Nixon's pusillanimity which led him to agree to giving a speech for which he is unprepared. It was Wells's conceit and indecent ambition that made him vulnerable to my encouragement towards disloyalty.

Stafford can be put in the same category as Nixon. He is, I recognize, not a bad man, but he has neither intelligence nor imagination. For too many years I have suffered his complacent drivel about his own success in heading a large company. He has even, on occasion, talked of the pleasure he gets from inhabiting the 'real world', or, in one of his more objectionable phrases, 'working at the coal face'. My father worked 'at the coal face' for a time when his firm was smashed through the economic incompetence of a government. He did labouring jobs for which he was unsuited and I saw too often the state of exhaustion and despair to which he was reduced. That expression from a fool in fancy clothes has driven me to rage. Cold rage. To fix Stafford's departure from a job he never deserved has been a pleasure.

Parkinson is different. He is an able man who has deserved better from me than he has received. I cannot hide from myself that some of the malice I have felt towards him has been a consequence of envy. He has more charm than I have, and, within his own sphere, probably as much ability. It is his misfortune that he became a sacrificial victim. I choose to blame the oafs who think that administrators like me are in some way inferior to people with technological skills. When I suggested to Parkinson that he should come to work on the administrative side I intended to do him a favour. Later I realized that I simply could not bear his competence in my own field. Had he succeeded he would have given ammunition to those who think that the skills of a good administrator can be picked up by anyone. I couldn't afford to let him succeed, and over the years I have come to hate him as the enemy of those who should be the true élite. What understanding do scientists have of the political dilemmas with which government has to grapple? What have they ever done but exacerbate those dilemmas by the construction of weapons for whose use they decline to take responsibility? Parkinson has had to suffer for the sins of his kind.

I don't have time to explain to you the plans I have made for bringing all these people to a murderous state. You would not, in any case, find the account edifying. You will probably rightly feel, despite my explanation, that I have become destructive for destruction's sake. That may well be the truth. I cannot, however, resist the temptation to see whether any one of these people has the gumption to hit back at me. I doubt it. I only hope, should it happen, that I see who it is that does it. In any case, my contingency suicide plans should provide some amusement for my staff over the next few days. I cannot think that I will be mourned.

With all good wishes,

Nicholas Clark

Amiss looked at his watch. Five minutes till the car was due to take them to the funeral. He dialled a number.

'How about a curry tonight?' he asked.

To receive a free catalog of Poisoned Pen Press titles, please
contact us in one of the following ways:

Phone: 1-800-421-3976
Facsimile: 1-480-949-1707
Email: info@poisonedpenpress.com
Website: www.poisonedpenpress.com

Poisoned Pen Press
6962 E. First Ave. Ste. 103
Scottsdale, AZ 85251